Scales and Scars

CIERRA GARDNER

NORTHWEST PINES PUBLISHING

This book is dedicated to all my Disney-loving, dirty-minded little Smut-A-Holics. Oh, we all know you will want more after this. But most importantly, this book is for my supporter Kendyl. You followed me over a year ago to await this book, and well, here it is! Enjoy!

Author's Note

This book contains the following elements:

- Violence
- Mention of death
- Death
- Family death
- Military flashbacks
- Sexual Harassment
- Medical scenes
- Adult language
- Explicit sex
- BDSM aspects (breath play, impact play)
- Workplace conflict
- Mention of MM
- Mental Health
- PTSD
- Childbirth

And let's be honest there is probably more so… enjoy.

Prologue 1

ZAZ

My best friends and I were stationed together, and we experienced as much happiness as possible, given the circumstances. War was never fun, but when you were with your family, it made it a little easier.

We were stationed in Africa, and I was elated. This was more home to me than the States. Unlike the men I served with, I held a secret that not even my best friend Takar knew.

I was a shifter, and my animal was a lion, not the commonly perceived wolf. So Africa was home. As a shifter, no matter the type, there was only one rule: keep our existence a secret.

Lying to my brothers was hard, but if they knew, it could cause issues not only for me but for others like me.

Don't get me wrong, I knew they would never tell a soul on purpose, but slipups could be costly. Unless there was a reason to tell them, they would never know.

Currently, we were sitting at the table waiting for our boss to give us our next orders. We were SEALs and had missions to uphold.

"Alright men, we have our orders," the General said as he burst into the room. He barked out our orders and handed me the file. "Plan your move, Commander."

"Yes, sir." I said.

I looked through the intel and came up with a plan. A pretty solid one, if I must say. Once I had an idea of the key players, I gave my orders and we headed out.

"Let's get this done," I said as my men took their positions.

We moved as one. Raf was in the hot zone, and myself and Takar were on the outside. Gunfire sounded as we approached.

Shit, we were made.

Without hesitation, we returned fire. I raised my hand after a bit and gave the cue to cease fire. When the gunfire stopped, the area was chillingly silent.

"Roll call," I said into our earpiece. Everyone replied except Takar.

Fuck.

"Fan out," I ordered.

What the fuck did I miss?

Who slipped by us?

I shook my head. This was not something I needed to figure out right now. Right now, I needed to find my missing man. I headed to his last-known position. My lion gave me his eyes and ears as I looked around.

Just to the right, I heard sounds of slicing and impact. I moved with haste to the area, holding off on calling my brothers.

My lion had this.

He exploded to the surface upon seeing Takar with fear in his eyes as he was beaten and stabbed by the enemy. The bad guys' eyes widened as my paws hit the ground in front of them. Before they could react, I snapped their necks and tossed them to the side.

Once my lion sensed no more threats, we turned to look at Takar. He was bleeding out, getting pale and even blue.

Shit, he was going to die unless…

No, I couldn't. Could I?

My lion grew impatient and moved on his own authority. He sank his teeth into Takar's neck and shoulder before clawing his back.

Takar shifted immediately, his lion trying to heal him. Using my dominant tone, given to a Mufassa to their direct line of cubs, I told his lion to only do just enough healing for him to live. We still had a secret to keep, one I could now share with my best friend.

Once he shifted back, I followed and radioed the rest of the men to us while I rendered aid to Takar. He would have a long recovery and definitely a lot of questions, which I would answer.

I was at his side when he woke up after surgery. My lion communicated with his, helping with his job to not scare the man he possessed and to not shift. A newly turned shifter can struggle with shifting and doing it in a hospital was not ideal.

It became clear his mind struggled with what exactly had happened. He remembered seeing a lion, but instead of it saving him, it attacked him. Trauma was a fickle thing that could alter memories.

Damn it.

When I tried to explain, he would go into a panic attack, PTSD evident. Unfortunately, his injuries disqualified him from active duty. If I had let his lion heal him, he would have been fine, but unfortunately, it was not possible.

Too many eyes on our missions.

The fact he was non-deployable could break him. Raf was also injured and ended up losing a kidney, so he was looking at a possible medical discharge. All signs pointed to both leaving the SEALs. Two of my best men gone because of one damn mission. Thankfully, not gone in death.

They confirmed in the following weeks that my two best men would be discharged.

As much as I hated to lose them, they were alive, and that's all that mattered. Now I have to tell them goodbye.

Fuck, I hated this.

"You two are the best. You will be missed. I am damn proud to be your commander and friend."

We embraced each other. I knew my men were hurting, especially Takar, who fought his lion, essentially blocking me. Despite his resistance, I wouldn't give up, and I knew neither would he. I'd found them good jobs through some connections, so I knew they would not struggle and would be able to stay together. As they left to board their flight, my lion whined, not wanting his "cub" to leave.

"I know," I whispered to myself.

Oh, how I knew.

Prologue 2

COVE

A beautiful sound of a woman singing surfed the ocean waves around us.

Shit.

A siren call.

I looked around to see who they were targeting. My heart dropped when I saw the massive ship a few miles ahead. Big ships meant lots of people on board, and they were very messy. My men and I took off at max speed, trying desperately to get to the ship before the siren did. As we got closer, I scanned the ship for entry points, weak points, and rescue boats.

Fuck.

This wasn't just any ship, it was an oil tanker, *Coil Cove Depot*. A wreck was bad enough, but this boat would kill not only humans but sea creatures and mermaids alike.

Utter devastation.

I never had to say a word to my warriors. We all knew what we were up against, and we knew odds were there would be lives lost on all sides. All we could do was try to lessen the death toll.

Out of the corner of my eye, I noticed the siren and rushed to her, my strongest warrior close behind. The others tried desperately to get the ship on course using the water, which is when I noticed Tilly using her tail to create waves to move the ship away from the boulders.

The worst part about this whole thing is the spell a siren casts with its call. The captain would never even know what was happening until it was too late. All his equipment would show they were on course.

As I was about to come into contact with the siren, Poseidon spoke to me through our link. "Some will die, many will live, a hero in the mix to save the masses. Sickness will come, death as well. But good will happen from this too."

The man loved his riddles.

Before I could process the meaning of the words, the ship collided with the boulder.

Shit. We were too late.

My trident stabbed through the siren, and the body decayed immediately.

When a siren died, they turned to sand and salt. The heart-shattering sound of Tilly's cry of sheer pain caught my attention.

Damn it.

When I looked around, I first saw the lifeboats in the water. The crew made it out. Thank Poseidon, that was one less thing to worry about.

Then I found Tilly. Blood seeped out of her tail.

Oh no.

Ignoring the oil coming at me, I swam to her with haste, and my men followed. "Let's get her to safety. We can't let her die. Without her, this would have ended far worse than it did."

My men filed beneath our friend and carried her the several-mile swim home. The medics immediately tended to Tilly as I went to debrief the MerKing.

Gods, I hope she will be okay.

"Cove, you have gone above and beyond as usual. For that, I

thank you. We lost thirty lives today, but it was not for nothing. Please go get checked by the MerDoc," the MerKing said. We called the mermaids with medical training MerDocs as a sign of respect for their position.

"Yes, Your Majesty."

My heart ached. So many lives lost, so many families destroyed, and I couldn't help but think it was my fault.

I didn't get there fast enough.

Fuck, I should have done more.

Once I was cleared of immediate issues by the MerDoc, I was told to follow up since I swam through the oil. A sense of defeat weighed me down as I got home and went to my room. My mate was immediately at my side.

"It's not your fault, Cove," my mate said soothingly.

I shook my head. She was my whole world, she and my unborn daughter were what I lived for. What I fought for.

"But it is. I…"

My wife's fingers brushed my lips, silencing me.

"*You* did everything in your power to change the outcome, and you did. So did Tilly."

There was no convincing me that it wasn't my fault, so I just dropped it. I had no fight left in me.

The following weeks, I stayed home with my family. I felt like shit physically and mentally. Every day, I would throw up, run a fever, and just shake.

"Honey, you need to see the MerDoc. Something isn't right," my mate said as she brushed her hand down my cheek. I reached up and clasped her hand in mine.

"I'm fine," I said dismissively.

I deserved everything that was happening to me. I failed my men and my people.

She glared at me, then winced in pain.

"Love, are you alright?"

After a few moments, she let out a winded breath. "It's time," was all she said.

Oh shit.

Things happened quickly. We made the call and soon MerDocs were all over the place. My mate writhed in pain, and I was powerless to help her.

Fuck, I hated this.

Several long hours later, a small cry filled the air. My heart soared as I saw my beautiful daughter. Her tail flipped and soon she was swimming into her mother's arms.

Perfection.

My life was complete, and so was my family. My little girl was the life of every room, and despite the recent loss our town had experienced, people were happy.

Hell, even I was happy. She was just what I needed.

"I need to go on land and get a few things. I want to teach our daughter to shift, but need the human necessities," my mate said. A groan of unease escaped my lips. This was not uncommon since our young were advanced and it was tradition for the mother to go to land shortly after giving birth "Don't worry. You have plenty of help from the neighbors. You will survive a few hours without me."

She kissed me passionately before pulling away. "I love you."

"I love you too," I replied.

She disappeared into the distance, leaving me with our daughter.

She was right. The neighbors helped a lot, and we went to see Tilly, who was improving. Things were looking good, and I was beginning to find my happiness.

When I finally got Aria to sleep, there was a knock on my door. I opened it to see the MerKing himself, his expression grim.

Oh no.

"Pearl?" I breathed. His eyes fell, and he nodded. I clenched my chest as I felt like I would explode from the heartache.

"She was killed by a drunk driver," he strained out in just a whisper.

I fell to the floor as my body just seemed to give up. A scream escaped my lips as my heart sank. My best friend, my mate, the love of my life was gone, and I was alone with our daughter.

"Not alone. Your village will always surround you," Poseidon said in my mind.

I screamed in my mind, unable to make a sound.

It certainly didn't feel like that, not now.

I coughed through my sobs, and my eyes widened as I noticed the blood on my hands. I looked up and saw the look of horror on my MerKing's face.

Before I could blink, I was in our hospital and Aria was under the care of the MerKing.

"Aria will be safe in the castle. You need to be checked, your daughter needs you to be healthy," the MerKing said.

The MerDocs ran test after test before coming back into the room. "The oil got into your system. I'm afraid you ingested a lethal amount. I wish I had better news. It appears you have some time. Hopefully, you will be able to see your daughter grow up, but there is no way to know for sure. It is all in the hands of Poseidon."

"No, I will see my daughter grow up. I owe it to her mother," I hissed with determination. The MerDoc nodded.

"I will check on the other survivors as well. We need to see if they have any issues. Who was your second?"

"His name is Kai," I growled.

Shit, that came out harshly. I smiled apologetically.

"Yes, of course," he responded.

Then, just like that, I was alone and left to my own thoughts.

I was dying.

Fuck me.

Chapter One

ARIA

The waves splashed against my tail as I sat on a rock just out of swimming distance from the shore. The beach buzzed with activity, and I wished I could join them.

Unfortunately, with so many people around, it was likely I would be spotted as I shifted, and that was the last thing anyone wanted.

I mean, the humans would love seeing a real live mermaid, but it would bring death and despair to my people.

The sky was a deep red and orange as the sun started to descend. The added purple made it that much more stunning. It also meant I needed to head back soon or I would miss dinner.

I let out a sigh to bid farewell to the land and turned to get off the rock.

Out of the corner of my eye, I saw someone who immediately took my breath away.

Ho-ly shit.

His body screamed for me to touch it. I wanted nothing more

than to trace my fingers across his built, but not overly muscular, body. He was in blue shorts and had a perfectly round ass.

Snap out of it!

What the hell, Aria?

Forcing my eyes up, I looked at his back as he turned to pick up a cooler. His black hair was in a messy bun on his head, allowing his scars to show. As I took him all in, I noticed the scars almost looked like claw marks going from left to right down his back.

Ouch. What the hell happened to this man?

When he turned back to me, I noticed his hair formed a V on his forehead to match the V that led to his…

Oh hell.

I forced my eyes up yet again, noticing his goatee brought out his sharp cheeks. My body tingled with a desire to be under this man.

Poseidon help me.

I needed to get out of here now before I exposed myself to everyone on the beach.

As I slipped into the water, I moved a little closer but still kept my distance. I felt a pull toward him, but a quick look around and I knew it wasn't safe.

Not right now.

I gasped when I watched his eyes shift to a greenish-golden color before turning back to the stunning gray color. Which also brought my attention to the scar over his eye.

Holy hell.

He pulled something out of his pocket and put it to his ear. A phone. I watched as his beautiful figure disappeared, and I fought the urge to go after him. What was that about? Despite my better judgment, I waited a bit to see if he came back.

He didn't.

Letting out a defeated sigh, I headed toward home.

Chapter Two

TAKAR

Watching the families at the beach was something I loved to do, along with listening to the sounds of the waves. I envied them, but it still brought me comfort being here. As I was enjoying the sounds and sights, I felt someone watching me. I was surprised I wasn't alarmed by it. If anything, it made me excited.

The hell?

I turned to see who it was, but saw no one. My mind tried to figure out where the person was. It's not like they could watch me from underwater. A person had to breathe. The only thing I could see was a rock just out of swimming distance.

Strange.

I was brought back to reality when my phone rang in my pocket. Letting out a groan, I answered it.

"What do you want?" My tone was harsh, as it usually was.

"Hey boss, some stuff came up with one of the workers. We need you to come back to the office," Raf said.

"And you can't take care of it?"

"No, boss, it has to be you."

Damn it.

"On my way."

If I had a flip phone, I would have slammed the damn thing shut. I was fucking done with work and now I had to go back and pick up everyone else's mess.

Raf was good at his job, but he could only do so much. Despite my asshole ways, I was the one who got things done. And I was a sweetheart compared to my boss.

The man only cared about money, cutting corners every chance he got. If I didn't do what I did, it would not end well for anyone.

This job was terrible, to say the least. Oil, in my opinion, was hurting people more than helping. Zaz got me and Raf these jobs and they paid the bills, so here we were. Wouldn't it be nice if bills paid themselves?

For fuck's sake, we were still trying to pick up the pieces after a catastrophic accident several years ago. We lost thousands, if not millions, of dollars in oil. The whole wreck seemed a little suspicious, but nothing anybody could ever prove.

Believe me, I tried.

The whole thing made Chad even greedier than he was before, wanting to make the money back by cutting corners every chance he had. Of course, I would never stand for it, so I always put up a fight.

Zaz said he never used to be like that, but he changed after the accident. If he had known, he would have arranged different jobs. Raf and I stayed to try to make it better, to do what we could to stop Chad from hurting people.

Most of the time, I did an okay job of winning the arguments with the man, but occasionally I would not succeed. When I could, I would do things behind his back and alter documents to make him think we did it his way. The man was clueless when it came to accounting, so it was fairly easy to do.

It took a few hours, but once I dealt with a very unhappy client and did some problem solving, I left the office and went to hang out with Raf at the club. I didn't mind clubs since my scar was harder to see in the poor lighting.

Raf used to just come and chill at my place on the reservation, but since my mom wanted to enjoy some alone time, I moved off the Rez to the beach, and we shared the place. Now that we lived together, it was more fun to go out. And to top it off, Raf was also the only one who knew my secret. The monster I caged inside of me. So he also knew when we needed to leave for everyone's safety.

As usual, women swarmed us as soon as we got inside. If only they knew how ugly I truly was. Normally I would take one home with me, then have my way with her all night before the sunlight showed my scar and she would tuck tail and run.

Tonight, I wasn't in the mood.

Despite not wanting to take a woman home, I needed a release.

I needed a girl on her knees sucking my cock. A small brunette came over with a seductive grin on her face. Without a word, I took her hand and led her to the back restroom. Once inside, I locked the door so that we were not interrupted.

Been there, done that.

"On your knees," I ordered.

She immediately dropped to her knees and looked up at me.

Oh fuck, now that was a view.

Though I preferred redheads.

With a quick movement, my pants dropped to the ground, exposing my fully erect cock. "Put those lips on my cock and suck me until I cum down your throat," I said, pointing the tip at her lips.

Without hesitation, she got to work.

I got pleasure from it, but not a lot. Something was missing, though I didn't know what. It was still enough to satisfy the need, but never fully satisfying. I shuddered as my orgasm reached the surface, and I exploded my release in her mouth.

Like a pro, she swallowed every last drop and looked up at me.

"You are dismissed."

She nodded and left the room, leaving me to clean up. For some unknown reason, the act made me feel so raw. It never had before.

What the hell was wrong with me?

First, someone was watching me, but no one was there, and now this.

Ugh.

The club wasn't far from my place, so I just shot Raf a text and headed back to the house to lie down. Though I wasn't able to sleep. I couldn't stop thinking about who could have been watching me on the beach and where they were.

Fuck me.

AHHHH!!

I fucking hated myself. I was scarred for life, and I didn't know if I could ever be happy again.

I was a soldier and fighting along with my brothers, and next thing I knew, I was a monster. A voice lived in my head, and I wanted so desperately for him to leave me the hell alone.

Not only that, but I had scars all over my body.

No matter what the doctors tried, nothing would make these constant reminders of my attack go away. If it was just the ones on my back, I could live with that, but the one over my eye made me look hideous.

Before the attack, I would go out and just be social. Hell, I was even a nice guy. But now I shut myself off and was a dick to everyone I talked to, everyone except Raf, my brother, who was also hurt the same day.

At this point, I didn't have a mirror in my home because whenever I looked in it, my body filled with hate. The red line, an unwanted trophy of my attack. The only place I found peace was the beach, so I headed there to enjoy the waves and salty air.

Chapter Three

ARIA

I like my privacy so I lived away from the rest of my clan.
During my many explorations, I found a cave near an inaccessible island. Too many rocks for a boat.

People could swim if they really wanted to, so I had a witch cast a spell to prevent the cave from being found by humans. When I told my dad about this place, he said it sounded like my mom's hideaway. He was too sick to come with me and find out.

I never knew my mom. She died right after I was born, but my dad and our MerKing made sure I knew who she was.

Whenever I went to land, my dad worried since my mom had been killed while visiting land. Originally, he refused to let me go at all, and I listened at first. But after a while, I started to feel I was being pulled to the land by an unseen force. My best friend would always say it was my mate.

Yeah, right.

That would mean my mate was a human, a rare occurrence. Land and sea don't mix well. But knowing the potential was there, I told my father, and he started letting me go as long as I was home for dinner.

"Aria." A familiar voice sounded in the distance as I approached my cave. I turned, knowing I would see my best friend Cora. I swayed my tail down and stopped my forward momentum as I looked around. It didn't take long to spot Cora waiting by the gate to my place.

"What's up?" I inquired as I swam over to her.

"Any luck on the mate front?"

I let out a sigh. My dad wanted me to find my mate so bad. Pretty sure he was holding on until I did, since the last thing he wants is for me to be alone. "No, not that I know of."

"Damn, I wanted something to make your dad feel a little better. He is restless today."

"Restless how?"

"He is getting sicker."

Shit.

My father was poisoned by toxic oil when a ship wrecked before he could stop it. Now, as a result, he was slowly dying.

"So, the poison is taking its toll?" I asked and got a nod in response.

Ugh, I hated this.

"Can you cover for me tomorrow?" I asked. Cora's lips fell into a deep frown.

"I guess. What are you planning on doing?"

"I need to go on land to talk to my witch friend. See if she can maybe help me find my mate somehow. If you're right, he spends his time on land, and I need to find him. Not just for me, but also for my father."

"Yeah, I will. Just check in, okay?"

"Of course."

After I dropped off today's finds, I headed over to my dad's bed and sat next to him. When my dad was a leader, he took no shit and accepted no excuses. People always told me stories of the fierce man he'd been.

I never saw that side of him. He retired soon after I was born and he became ill. He still barked orders and was respected. I always got the teddy bear version, I guess.

Though he was also nice to Kai, his right-hand man. He was young when the attack happened. He was also the closest to the spill. Like my father, he was slowly dying, though not as quickly.

As I laid my head next to my dad, his fingers brushed through my hair. His touch brought me so much comfort, and mine, him. He always said I looked just like my mom and sometimes, looking in my eyes, he could see her smiling back at him.

"Sweetheart, you will meet your mate tomorrow. Whatever you are planning to do tomorrow has set your course. He is lost, and you will have to help him, teach him. But he will be yours. Poseidon tells me so."

What the?

My dad would often get messages from our god, and this helped us stay alive. Once I find my mate, the ability is supposed to be passed to me or my mate, depending on who Poseidon deems worthy. Yet another reason for me to find him soon. If my father died, our connection with our God would be severed, and it would devastate Merkind.

I really hoped the words my dad spoke were true. We needed this. My dad was suffering, and it was time he found his peace. Even if that meant he left this life.

As I swam home, I wondered if I really would find my mate tomorrow and what my dad meant by "he is lost, and you will have to help him."

Damn riddles.

Chapter Four

TAKAR

As soon as I was up, I headed to the beach. I wasn't completely sure why, but I was being pulled there, like I needed to be there for whatever reason.

Could it be to find the mystery person who was watching me, or was it something else?

Fuck, I don't know.

I breathed deeply, taking in the clean air and quiet. It was too early for the beachgoers to be here so I was alone.

My phone vibrated in my pocket, bringing me back to the present.

"Hello," I answered.

"T, I just got a phone call. You're not going to like this," Raf said.

"What did our boss do now?"

"It's not about him. It's Zaz."

Shit. "What about Zaz?"

"He is MIA."

No! How?

Zaz was the best, and if he was missing, then who the hell would be able to save him?

Damn it.

I had the urge to punch something, but I was on the beach. Nothing to get this anger and worry out of me. In an effort to calm myself, I took a deep breath. "What do we know?"

"Unfortunately, not much. All I know is he was on a mission that went south. After all was said and done, everyone returned except Zaz. They're currently trying to locate him. But you and I both know how things can get over there."

I dropped to my knees and then down until I was sitting with my head between my legs.

I wanted to scream, but no sound came out.

Raf hung up. He knew I needed time to process the news, and it was best to leave me alone for now.

"This can't be happening," I muttered to myself. Tears threatened to break free, and my barriers started to crumble.

Then I felt it.

Those eyes were on me again.

My body tingled in anticipation as whoever it was edged closer. Feet stopped just in front of me, and I slowly looked up.

Holy shit, she was stunning.

Her seashell and seahorse bikini fit her perfectly, and her fire-red hair practically glowed in the morning sunlight. The urge to touch her, to kiss her, hell, to fuck her, was strong. What the fuck was happening?

By some miracle, I fought the urge.

I was no good for her. She was too beautiful to be with a monster like me. Hell, I'm not even good for myself.

I wanted to scream as I fought for control, my cock taking an interest in the woman standing in front of me.

"I don't know who you are, but I'm not interested," I said harshly, looking down to dilute the urge.

"You seemed upset, and I wanted to make sure you were okay. I know you don't know me, but..."

When she spoke, my heart nearly melted. It made me warm inside, and I struggled all over again.

No. I would not do this.

Moving faster than should have been possible, I stood until I was towering over her short frame. But it left me closer to her, almost touching her. My eyes met hers, and I was surprised not to see fear.

Snap out of it, damn it.

"You're right, you don't know me. You would be wise to stay away from me," I growled. Her responding frown sent a pain through my chest, but I pushed it aside.

I was broken and carried a lot of demons with me every day, not to mention the beast inside of me. To my surprise, she reached up and touched my chest.

What the hell?

Something about her touch made my muscles relax. I jerked back, almost losing control. I turned on my heels and practically ran to the office.

If I had stayed, I would have lost control. Leaving was the right thing.

Fuck.

My heart ached as I made it to my car. So many questions swarmed my mind.

Mainly, what the hell was happening?

I rubbed my temples, trying to erase the image of her perfect face, her banging body that should only belong to a damn goddess.

Shit.

I didn't even know her name, but now she seemed to take up all my thoughts. Soon, the images turned to Zaz. He was bloody, dead, or running for his life.

God, I hope he is okay.

If he wasn't okay, I honestly didn't know if I could continue through life. Then she came back to my mind, and I grasped my chest.

Part of me wanted to know her, but I was scarred, broken, distant, and completely unworthy.

I WAS a damn mess when I got the news about Zaz. The emotions that ran through me were like a storm cloud just waiting to become an uncontrolled tornado. I knew one wrong thing and my temper would flare, so I didn't go to work.

My boss could fuck off.

For fuck's sake, Zaz had saved my damn life, and now I was powerless to save him. I desperately needed him to be okay. My lion was restless and demanding to break through. Then she came to mind. Even the thought of her calmed me.

As I showered, her image flashed through my mind, and I let my imagination take hold as I stroked my cock. Pictured myself buried inside of her, pleasing her like she deserved until we both found our release. I fisted my pulsing cock and jerked when my cum jetted out. I moaned, "Red."

While my body and mind came down from their high, my mind filled with hatred, not for her, but for myself.

How could I think of her like that?

I didn't deserve her.

I didn't know what this pull was, but it was something beyond my control. But I could control myself and what I did. The water ran cold, and I headed to the gym. I needed to let off some steam.

Chapter Five

ARIA

When he jerked away from me and ran back to the city, leaving me alone on the beach, an emptiness filled me. What was that?

Whatever it was, I couldn't dwell on it. Hopefully Ursa could help me figure out everything. As soon as I got there, I sat in the chair directly across from her, and she looked at me with her eyebrow raised as she seemed to stare into my soul.

Hell, maybe she was. She was a witch, for crying out loud.

"You look rough. What happened?"

"Well, long story short, I saw a guy on the beach. He was harsh and so unforgiving, but…something about him just won't let me give up on him. It's like I have to be near him."

"Hold that thought," she said as she got up and grabbed her crystal ball. She chanted and swirled her hands until it started to emit light. Her eyes widened and then locked with mine. "The scarred and the scaled will join. Together they will be strong and powerful to lead the land and sea in the ways of Poseidon."

What the hell? More damn riddles. Though this one wasn't as hard to figure out as some have been.

The man from the beach was my mate. Slash was mine. But he ran away from me, so now what the hell was I supposed to do?

"Damaged and lost. He needs to find himself, and she holds the key," she added.

I groaned and held my head between my hands. This was not going to be easy, was it? Ugh, figures.

Obviously, I needed to see him again, but something told me right now was not the time, so I stayed and hung out with my friend. One of the many topics we discussed was the words she spoke.

What could they mean? Other than the obvious, that is.

We had a blast at lunch, then enjoyed a movie before heading back to her place until I had to go to see my father. Not to mention Cora would want to know what happened right away. Her mom cared for my father as a nurse, so we became friends growing up and, well, now she helps her mom with my dad.

Her father died the day of the wreck, so my father was always there for her, in his place. Making us practically sisters.

Ursa and I said our goodbyes, and I left for the ocean to shift back. Before leaving, I sat on my rock and took in the beautiful sun.

I lowered myself into the water and prepared to dive when I felt his presence. I flicked my tail beneath me for balance and turned to look. My eyes locked with his, and he took a few steps toward me but stopped at the wave's edge.

My body vibrated as Cora called to me through the water.

Shit, something was wrong.

I wanted so badly to go to my scarred man, but my father might need me. In an effort to acknowledge him, I waved before I submerged myself in the depths of the sea and swam hastily home.

If he was my mate, my leaving that way probably hurt. I mean, it hurt me.

As I approached, Cora waved me over.

"What is it?" I asked.

"Your father. He had another episode."

Crap.

For a while now, my dad would get episodes where he would hallucinate, scream, yell, and break things. It could be terrifying. This was his third one in a week compared to one to two times a month, which meant he was getting worse.

I knew my father had to die at some point, but it didn't make it any easier. He was my best friend. In the end, I also don't want him to live only to suffer. He was in pain.

"How is he now?" I asked.

"He's stabilized and sleeping. We had to knock him out with meds this time."

Based on what the MerDocs said, this would happen close to the end. He would slowly lose his mind until he died. I sighed. *Ugh, I hate this.*

Cora embraced me, then pulled back. "Did you meet your mate today like your father said?"

"I think so. He was walking up to the beach when you called. So we didn't get to talk, but we had a moment earlier when I first got to land."

She raised an eyebrow. "A moment?"

"I touched him and literally felt his muscles relax. Then he said I would be wise to stay away. But I think he feels it as much as I do, just has some demons."

"Did you at least get his name?"

"No, I didn't, but he has a scar on his back and over his eye. I can spot him if I see him. Not to mention sense him."

As soon as I thought about him, all I could see was him.

His sexy, perfectly toned body.

Poseidon have mercy. If I was in my human form, my panties would be soaked.

"Tomorrow I will go with you. We can find him together, and maybe I can help."

"I-I don't know. Don't get me wrong, I know you make a good wingwoman, but I get a vibe that he wouldn't respond well."

I mean, he was already standoffish, and I didn't want to scare him. Cora could be a bit wild.

"I'll keep my distance when he is close if I need to, but I got to see this mate of yours, since he has you drooling."

I shrugged heavily. "I guess."

When my friend wanted something, she got it. So this was a losing battle. After I visited my dad, I headed home and went to bed. I had no idea how things would go tomorrow, but I knew one thing for sure.

I needed to see him.

<h1 style="text-align:center">Chapter Six</h1>

ARIA

When Cora and I made it close to the beach, she turned to me. "Where do you normally see him?"

"The rock by the north shore. I can hide from the humans there."

She nodded as we made our way there. We clambered onto the rock and looked around, still in our mermaid forms.

"Is he here?"

Even though I knew he wasn't—I couldn't feel him—I still looked. My heart ached at the thought that he wouldn't be here.

Damn.

"No, but it's early," I said, more to myself but still answering her question.

Just as the words came out, my body tingled, and I felt pulled to the shore. This time when I looked, I saw him. Not only that, but he was looking right at us. My body jolted as our gazes seemed to lock onto each other.

Shiiiit. He was sexy as hell.

"That's him?" Cora asked. I nodded, since my throat was far too dry to even attempt to speak. "Damn girl, he is hot as hell."

My cheeks heated, and I motioned for us to go to shore so we could shift before too many more people came to the water. This time, I wore a teal swimsuit with an overskirt that matched Cora's yellow one.

As we approached, he turned to us. I could have sworn I saw his mouth twitch with the hint of a smile.

Impossible.

His face was hard and unwelcoming, just like before. I needed to get through to him somehow.

As we got closer, I could have sworn I heard him growl.

Shit.

The first thought I had was that he didn't like that I wasn't alone. I put my hand out to stop Cora. "Let me go to him alone."

Her wary eyes glanced between us. "Are you sure?"

Her concern was evident in her tone. I nodded. She sat on the beach and lay in the sand. She was close, but not out of sight. That was the best I could do.

I moved toward Slash, who watched me intently as I approached. Despite my urge and desire to be closer, I stopped at a respectful distance.

Patience, Aria.

Chapter Seven

TAKAR

I headed to the beach, hoping to see her, but also hoping she wouldn't be there.

Honestly, this battle with myself was getting old, but I just couldn't seem to stop. I wanted her so damn bad, but I was not okay, physically or mentally. So how would I even manage to be a fraction of what she deserved?

"She can help, you know. You just have to let her in," my lion said. I shook my head. I haven't heard my lion's voice in so long, not since I stopped shifting, *refused* to let myself shift. Since I hated what I had become, I shut my lion out.

I heard another voice, not that of my lion but still somehow familiar. "Just let it be."

My brain whirled at what that meant. I shook my head and shut myself off, as I usually did. This was all too much.

As soon as I arrived at the beach, I saw her. But she wasn't alone. I wanted her to myself but was also glad she wasn't alone.

Honestly, I didn't know how in control I was. I didn't trust myself with her. Somehow, I would hurt her. I just knew it. Especially since I was bigger than she was. I was a monster.

A growl escaped my lips as the two approached me. The pair stopped, and Red whispered something to her friend. With some glances back and forth, she submitted and sat in the sand as Red continued toward me.

I looked her up and down as she stopped just out of reach.

Fuck, she was fine as hell.

"Hi," she said softly, and I swear I melted right there. Her voice was like a damn drug.

"Hi," I said gruffly. I fidgeted as I fought the urge to run.

"Please don't go," she practically begged.

I moved my eyes to hers in disbelief. Did she really want to be near me?

"I'm not good for you. I—"

The sentence fell short as she moved in closer and placed her soft hand on my chest, making my body relax immediately. I automatically closed my eyes and took a deep breath, wanting to savor this moment before it ended.

"Let me decide what is good for me," she responded in a soft yet stern tone.

"But—"

She silenced me with a finger placed on my lips. "Do you feel the pull?"

Of course I did. I wasn't dead.

I hesitated a moment, then nodded.

"It's called a mate pull. The goddess and gods, for whatever reason, matched us together," she said.

The what? Who?

Fuck, it didn't matter.

I was not worthy.

"I'm a monster," I snarled. I expected her to jump and back up, but instead she leaned into my chest. On instinct my arms wrapped around her waist.

Fuck, this was heaven.

"You are no monster in my eyes," she said, looking up.

"I look hideous. My scars, they consume me. And I turn into a—" I was cut off again and stunned silent as her fingers traced my scar. My body automatically leaned into the touch. Pretty sure my lion purred, hell, I think even *I* purred.

Fucking purred like a damn cat. Yes, I know lions don't actually purr. Hum might be a better description, but it sounded like a purr to me. Her cool touch made me crave more.

My lion was taking control, and I didn't even mind. What was happening to me?

Then she shocked me again.

"I love your scars. I think they make you sexier somehow."

Oh hell. The air filled with a sweet smell, and my lion seemed to lose himself. Was she aroused?

"I don't deserve you."

She rolled her eyes, and my cock twitched at the sight.

"Let me decide that."

When she kissed my scar, my lion came forward despite my efforts.

"Mate, mine," he growled.

Next thing I knew, I was forehead to forehead with her, her sweet scent driving me wild with desire.

I was done for. I needed her like I needed my next breath.

"You and your friend want to come have dinner with me. I have a friend I can introduce her to and even out the numbers. Right now I have to go to work, but meet me here at six. Wear something nice," I practically ordered.

Based on the way she clutched her thighs together and the sweet smell that filled the air, I think she liked it.

"We will be here," she breathed. "But first, what is your name? I keep calling you Slash."

I tensed at the name, then my lion came forward. "She loves our scars."

As much as I hated to admit it, he was right. I relaxed as she spoke again.

"I'm sorry." She looked so heartbroken and scared. Not of me, but that she had said something bad.

Well, that just wouldn't do.

Moving on instinct, I brushed my lips against hers, catching her weight as she seemed to collapse. Hell, I struggled with staying upright. Everything about the kiss felt so right and filled me to capacity with pleasure.

"Don't be," I whispered. "Takar."

"Takar."

Holy shit. The sound of my name coming from her lips was porn-worthy.

"Yours?" I inquired.

"Aria."

I whispered her name before I claimed her lips again. Honestly, I could kiss her all day.

My phone vibrated aggressively in my pocket. I held back my growl. This had better be good.

"Speak," I said harshly into the phone. I hated that we were interrupted but also thankful. If the call hadn't come, I had no clue how far I would have taken this.

When I saw Aria flinch, I moved closer to her on instinct. Like I knew just being close could solve a lot of issues. Could it really help me?

"Boss, remember you have a meeting in an hour?"

"I'll be there." I sighed as I looked down at Aria and smiled slightly.

Fucking smiled. Damn.

"Before you go, you are coming to dinner tonight. I have found two beautiful ladies to join us."

"Sure thing, boss. Is this like a date or…?"

"I don't know…" I muttered.

Was it?

"Alright, well, I'm in."

"Good. See you in a bit."

I hung up and leaned down a bit more to brush my lips

against hers again. I just couldn't help myself. Now that I had a taste, I needed it. Just as I was losing myself to her, I jerked back.

Shit.

I needed to get to my meeting, or my boss would have my hide.

"I have to go." I spun and left.

Chapter Eight

ARIA

"How did it go?" Cora asked, making me jump. "It looked like it went alright."

"Girl, you scared the shit out of me. But I guess it went well despite the hasty getaway. I know his name, and we have plans tonight. Which means some shopping is in order," I said, feeling a little bit more excited. Cora beamed.

This girl loved to shop.

We headed to Ursa's place and grabbed the bank cards we stored there. You know water damage is a thing with human realm stuff. Ursa smiled as we came in.

"Mates times two tonight anew. You will go in four, but come out two."

What the hell was that supposed to mean?

Cora and I shared a look before we turned back to Ursa. She didn't say anything else while we grabbed our stuff and headed out. We had known her long enough to know that if she were going to elaborate, she would. Otherwise, it was no use asking questions.

Hell, sometimes she didn't have a clue.

Once outside and heading down the street, I turned to Cora. "What do you think she meant?"

"I dunno."

"I mean, I know she gets visions and hears messages from beyond, but that was odd even for her."

"Agreed."

We stopped at a small store along the beach and looked around. The clothes were cute with very summer vibes. Which wasn't a bad thing, but we needed club-worthy. Just as we were about to give up, something in the back corner caught my eye.

A purple dress that glittered in the sunrays caught my attention.

When I tried it on, it came to about mid thigh and swooped down the chest and had a bare back. The sales woman handed me some silver heels to complete the look. Then I saw Cora in a dress similar to mine but with more length.

She looked stunning.

We made our purchases, then headed to lunch. Mermaids preferred fish and seaweed, but sometimes human food was a nice change.

After we enjoyed our food, we went to get our hair done. Since we weren't on land a lot, we never invested in anything except clothes. If we wanted to go out, we hired professionals to style us.

We were in our dresses but carried our shoes as we walked along the beach. I glanced at my watch and smiled.

The guys would be here any minute.

Chapter Nine

TAKAR

As I pushed through the people protesting the oil industry out front, I thought about Aria. She was absolutely stunning, and being away from her made me restless.

The crowd of protesters seemed angrier and larger than normal, and I didn't blame them. But unlike them, I was actively trying to make changes from the inside instead of holding a damn sign and yelling.

You want change, then take action. Don't demand others to do it for you.

Lazy pricks.

I practically tore the door off its hinges as I entered my office and sat down at my solid red oak desk. My meeting came and went. It was a pointless meeting that accomplished absolutely nothing, just like the protesters outside.

Absently, my fingers grazed my lips where hers had been, wanting the sensation to return.

Fuck, she tasted so damn good.

Raf came in the door and sat across from me, staring at my

fingers. He looked at me with a knowing smirk. "You kiss someone?"

Gee, what gave you that idea?

I slammed my hand down and cleared my throat, glaring at him.

"Hey no judgment here. You deserve to be happy."

"Do I though? I am not exactly fit for a relationship," I groaned as I leaned back. Raf leaned forward onto my desk.

"Yes, you do," he said sternly. "Look, I was not there when everything happened, but I do know it does not define you. Unless you let it."

The man had a point, but I couldn't help the way I felt. This would not be easy for me or for her. Could she handle that?

He dropped the subject, and I did my orders and paperwork, which he filed and documented as we went. Once we were done, we headed to my place, grabbed some fresh clothes for dinner, and headed out.

"Where are we meeting them?"

"The beach."

Chapter Ten

ARIA

When I felt his presence, I looked up and saw him standing next to a man who was almost as tall as he was. Cora made an odd noise, making me snap my head around to look at her.

Honestly, I was probably looking at her like she was a foreign alien.

"Cora?" I asked.

"Mate," she whispered. I looked between her and the man standing next to Slash.

Odd. He was human.

One look at him and I could tell he felt it just as much as she did. I noticed Slash looking between the two with curiosity and confusion in his eyes. I motioned with my head for him to walk over to the side, to me. Which he did without hesitation. Not only that, but he was right in front of me, practically no distance between us.

"What's happening?" he whispered.

"It appears they are mates," I said, looking into his eyes. A hint of a smirk crossed his lips, but the confusion was still evident.

"But Raf is human," he mumbled.

"Are you not?" I asked softly. Ursa implied he might not be, but still we hadn't talked about it, or me, for that matter.

He tensed up, and I reached my hand to his chest, immediately relaxing him. He reached around my waist and pulled me close.

Heaven.

"No," he said curtly. "Are you?"

"I'm a mermaid shifter."

He nodded in response. I wanted so desperately to ask what he shifted into, but something told me not to push the subject right now. We watched as Cora and Raf met for the first time and seemed to hit it off with no hesitation.

A pang of jealousy hit me.

This was everything I wanted. They accepted each other, and I knew she would not be coming home with me tonight. Until he was marked, he had to stay on land. Once marked, he would be able to shift.

A sigh escaped my lips before I realized I was doing it. I immediately felt Slash's eyes on me.

"Let's get going," I whispered as I turned to walk to the city.

Slash pulled me to him, making me crash into his chest. He put his finger under my chin and tilted my head to face him. I looked down, refusing to make eye contact.

But my body sure as hell noticed the action. Yes, please.

"What's wrong?" he asked in a harsh tone. I flinched instinctively. He brushed his hand over my face, and I relaxed into his hand before shaking my head, not wanting to answer his question.

A tear escaped, betraying me. He brushed it away with his thumb, then brought his lips to mine.

"Red, talk to me." His tone was almost pleading.

"It's stupid really," I muttered.

"Tell me."

I looked away, still not able to make eye contact. "It's just that…they are…so accepting of each other so easily," I said so low I could barely hear myself. But I knew he heard me. He put his fingers back under my chin so he could look me in the eye.

"I'm sorry, Red. I-I am broken, I don't deserve…"

I put my lips to his, and he wrapped himself around me. It wasn't long before I lost myself in the kiss. When he pulled away, both of us were breathless.

"You are not broken. We are fated together for a reason. Lean on me and we will figure it out. Together."

I could practically hear his mind working to process my words.

"Okay…" Then he pulled me up into another kiss. This one was different, deeper, and had more passion, no more resistance behind it. I melted into the kiss and got lost in his grasp.

When he pulled away, I noticed a slight smile on his lips.

A genuine smile.

"Better?" he asked.

I nodded, still trying to regulate my breathing.

"Much better."

He intertwined our hands, and he took a step back to look me up and down. "You look absolutely stunning, Red."

My cheeks heated at the compliment and the nickname.

"Red?"

"Your hair," he said as his hand brushed through my strands. "I love it, it's you."

I sometimes hated how red my hair was, but he liked it, much like I liked his scars. Somehow, we loved each other's insecurities. It was so perfectly fairytale that it was nauseating.

With his hand in mine, we walked up to Cora and Raf, who broke their embrace as we approached. It felt so nice, so natural, having my hand in his.

Chapter Eleven

TAKAR

Throughout dinner, my hand rested on Red's thigh. She was on my right, so I forced myself to eat with my left hand. It was almost like I needed to touch her. Next time, if there was one, I would sit with her on my lap.

Cora seemed very nice and, of course, protective of her best friend. She made sure to give the "you hurt her, you die" threat. I definitely didn't want to hurt Aria, but could I promise that and be truthful?

I don't know, so all I did was smile.

Being here with my best friend, Red, and her best friend felt so right, and as the night went on, my lion purred in my mind. I was still pushing him back, though not as much as before. We were content, and I honestly didn't want it to end.

"Why don't you stay with me tonight? I get the feeling Cora is not going home, and I don't like the idea of the night ending or you going home alone," I said before I could overthink it.

The thought of her alone did not sit well with me or my lion.

Plus, judging by the groaning happening across the table, Cora and Raf weren't going to be apart tonight.

Red's smile made me smile automatically and sent a surge of electricity through me.

"I'd love that."

Her soft voice filled me with happiness. I looked her up and down, desire flowing through me.

Hmmm.

Cora and Raf took off at one point. We stayed behind and ate some cheesecake before heading out. As we made our way to my place, my lion spoke to me.

"Something is upsetting our mate." His voice was almost a growl.

I looked at her and could see something was indeed off. Shit.

"Is something wrong?"

"It's nothing."

Her dismissive tone angered me. I didn't want to lose control, so I used the frustration and pinned her to the wall. As soon as I did, her scent flared and I smelled her sweet arousal.

Fuck.

My lion roared in my mind as I spoke. "It's not nothing. I can feel you are upset about something, just as much as I can smell how much you want me right now."

Her responding blush made my cock twitch.

Holy hell.

"I just… I want what Cora has," she blurted.

I could feel how much she hated what she was saying, almost like she felt stupid for even thinking about it. Then my heart broke at the realization of the words.

I was hurting her again, damn it.

"I-I wish I could be that for you, but I…"

Her lips met mine, and I moved my body against hers, removing the gap. She pulled back but kept her hand on the back of my neck, ready to pull me into her.

"You deserve this. You deserve to be happy despite what you think," she snarled.

Her free hand brushed against my already hard cock, and my lion roared.

Fuck. That's it.

I needed her, and I needed her now.

I scooped my hands under her perfect ass, picking her up. She wrapped her legs around me. Without a second thought, I brought her to my room and put her on my bed.

"I don't know about that, but I do know I can smell your arousal and I need to be inside of you," I growled as my lion purred in my mind. He was practically prancing in anticipation of being with our mate.

I questioned if this was right, but her pleading moan made me lose myself in her arousal. Losing all of my control, I practically ripped off her clothes. My eyes raked up and down her now-naked body.

Fuck, she was perfect.

I kissed every inch of her and made my way to her perfect pussy. My lion growled when I found just how soaked she was for me. I cupped her wetness and purred, "So wet for me."

I inserted my fingers into her core, my tongue flicking at her nub. The sight of her gripping the sheets in response was intoxicating.

As I worked my fingers in and out of her hot channel, my cock throbbed in anticipation of being inside her. But right now, I wanted to pleasure her.

Her moans filled the empty room as she writhed under my touch. Pre-cum leaked from my tip, and I pinched the base of my cock before I came all over the place.

I added more fingers and moved them in and out with haste, then dove to lick and nip at her bud. Going on instinct, I worked her inside and out until I felt her warm cum on my tongue as she moaned my name.

Fuck.

Not wanting to waste a single drop, I licked my lips as I came up from between her legs. I smiled devilishly at her.

She was so damn delicious, and now I wanted so much more.

Standing up, I quickly disposed of my clothes, which suddenly felt constricting. Her eyes bulged when my erection came into view.

One benefit of being a lion shifter was my cock grew quite a bit. It was big to begin with, but now it was even larger. Not to mention, nothing was small about me in general.

"Don't worry, Red. I'll go slow."

I positioned myself so my tip was at her entrance and looked her in the eye, making sure she was okay. Her hands gripped my hips, pulling me closer. She gasped as my tip entered her heat. Her grip moved to my arms. I fought the urge to just plunge into her, moving slowly, letting her adjust.

Once I hit the hilt, I let out a deep moan. "Fuck, Red, you are so tight."

I stayed there a minute while I fought off my orgasm.

She circled her hips, and my body seemed to ignite with fire, passion to be with her. I pulled out a few inches, then snapped my hips, plunging my length back into her heat.

Oh God.

Her sweet moans made my head spin, and my movements became faster as my hands wandered her body, making their way to her perfect nipples.

When she dug her nails into my back, my lion purred. Wanting to be deeper inside her, I wrapped my arms around her and pushed her down with each thrust.

"Slash," she moaned as I felt her walls tighten around my cock.

Oh fuck. My eyes crossed from the pleasure.

"Fuck, Red," I growled as my orgasm rushed to the surface and I came deep inside her hot channel. My body convulsed as more and more cum seemed to come out of my balls.

Jesus, where the fuck was I keeping all this cum?

When her walls finished milking my essence from the depths of my balls, I collapsed onto the bed next to her as I tried desperately to catch my breath. I smiled when she immediately curled into me and I wrapped my arms around her, still needing to be close.

Fucking heaven.

Chapter Twelve

TAKAR

I lost control and had sex with Red. Don't get me wrong, I didn't regret being with her, but I couldn't help but feel like I had done something wrong.

I couldn't maintain this, could I?

"That was…"

What was the word?

It wasn't a mistake, but it was something.

"Perfect," she whispered before I could come up with the word.

Perfect.

The word felt right. She was perfect and made for me. Why the hell was I denying this?

"Of course she is perfect. She is made for us. If you just let her in, she will help you," my lion said.

"Yeah," I agreed, both to her and my lion. I purred as she snuggled into me. When she propped herself up, I grew anxious.

Panic coursed through me, and I placed my hands on her

hips, essentially calming myself. She responded by swiftly getting up and straddling me.

"What do you turn into when you shift?" She almost sounded scared to ask me. My body tensed, and I regretted it instantly when she leaned away slightly.

Shit.

Through what I assumed was the mate pull, I could feel she really didn't care. She just wanted to know me. I, however, did not argue with her straddling me, nor did my cock.

"Lion," I whispered as I looked away. I couldn't handle her rejection.

She was silent, so I chanced a look. Her wide smile threw me off, but I continued. "I told you I was a monster, a lion, and you are smiling?"

This only made her smile more before she leaned down and claimed my lips with hers. I moaned and my heart soared as this was her accepting me for what I was. Part of me wondered if that would still be the case if she ever saw my lion, but that was for another day.

She pulled away and looked me in the eyes.

"My favorite animal is a lion."

No fucking way.

I tilted my head to the side and smiled. Part of me wondered if she was lying, but something told me she wasn't. "Really?"

When she confirmed, desire flowed through me, and I flipped her so she was under me again.

"She accepts us," my lion said with glee. "I want her to touch me. Let me out, let me be with my mate."

"My lion would love to meet you. He is begging me to let him out, especially now."

"I would love that. And I will show you my mermaid form."

I nodded. I wasn't sure if showing her my lion was a good idea, but the thought of her as a mermaid filled me with desire.

Did she feel the same about seeing me?

"Does your lion have their own voice?"

I was thrown off by the question, but I nodded. Not only was she accepting me, but she wanted to know more, understand me, understand us. Fuck, she was perfect.

And I needed her.

I needed to be inside her again.

"Enough with the questions," I growled seductively. "I want to be deep inside you."

I touched my cock to her wetness, and she moaned. Taking a chance, I let my lion forward slightly as I plunged into her until my balls were pressed against her perfect ass. My lion roared as her nails dug into my skin, leaving marks.

Shit, this was going to be over quickly.

My thrusts became erratic as I came close to orgasm.

Oh God.

My hand flew down to her clit, and I pressed down as my back went ramrod straight. My orgasm exploded through me.

Her screams filled the room as her walls strangled my twitching cock. Once I ensured every drop of my cum was deep inside her, I lay down next to her. When she moved to snuggle into my chest, her pussy brushed against me and my cock stiffened again.

Fucking hell.

"Again? How?" she asked with some alarm in her voice.

Oh, if only she knew.

I chuckled into the crook of her neck. "Lions can mate ten times an hour," I said, then pulled her into a soft, passionate kiss. "Don't worry, Red, we won't go ten times unless you want to."

"Maybe just one more."

Her seductive tone sent me over the edge. Oh fuck, don't have to tell me twice.

I chuckled and guided her until my shaft was deep inside her core again as she sat on top of me. She bounced on my cock, and my hands moved to her hips as I watched her breasts jiggle with every move.

Oh god, so damn perfect.

I moved my hands and grabbed her nipples, eliciting an intoxicating moan.

Using my hips, I bucked until she leaned over me. Then, taking the opportunity, I nipped at her breast as I thrust into her while she rode my cock like a cowgirl. She circled her hips, and my eyes rolled from ecstasy.

Holy shit. She knew how to move.

"Red, I'm going to—" I couldn't even finish the sentence before my body tensed and I came deep inside of her again as my head slammed back onto the bed. The sensation of her own orgasm made my release last longer.

I laid her next to me and moved down to her pussy. She was dripping all over the sheets with our juices. So fucking hot.

Time for a snack.

She gasped as I licked and sucked every last drop, teasing her clit as I did. I was in heaven, and I never wanted this to end.

Chapter Thirteen

TAKAR

Twelve times.

Holy shit, I can't believe I managed that. Granted, it was over the course of the whole night, but still.

The amount of satisfaction that filled me from head to toe was mind-boggling. My cock made it known it could go more, but the rest of me was exhausted, and honestly, so was Red.

A groan filled the room, and I snapped my eyes open and instinctually wrapped my arms around her. Then a thought hit me.

She was a virgin, I felt her hymen break, and I was far from gentle with her. Shit.

"You feeling sore?" I mumbled into her neck as I took in her sweet scent.

"Yes," she whined.

"Sorry," I whispered.

I was sorry, but at the same time, I wasn't. I'd do it all again.

Hearing her voice and smelling her was making me question whether I should continue to fight my nature or let this happen.

Fuck.

I don't know. With her right here, I couldn't think straight. For now, I would just enjoy the moment.

"Don't be," she said, and I couldn't help but chuckle at her tone. She was breathy as hell, and the next thing I knew, I could smell her arousal all over again.

Oh my fuck.

"That didn't take much," I teased. She turned to me and smiled.

"You are my mate. What did you expect?" she retorted, and I couldn't help but smirk. "Besides, the hard cock poking into my belly tells me you feel the same."

I rolled my eyes. "You caught me there."

Her lips crashed into mine with fierce abandon, and I immediately opened to her.

She moaned as I reached down to her folds, ready to please her all over again. My cock ached to be deep inside her again and was leaking profusely. The lust trance I was in snapped when my phone rang on the bedside table.

Fucking hell.

When I answered, I didn't say anything. I just growled my displeasure at being interrupted.

"Easy T. You damn well know I don't want to be calling either. Shit, my mate is a damn firecracker in the bedroom, and I want to be balls deep, just like you want to be with your mate. But you are needed in the office ASAP."

Red was making it hard as hell to concentrate as her lips wrapped around my aching tip.

I practically had to bite my tongue to avoid moaning. Though based on the heavy breathing on the other end of the phone, Raf was having the same issue. Except he was the one doing all the talking.

After he finished giving me the rundown of the situation, I slammed the phone down in time for my orgasm to explode through me.

"Shit, Red," I moaned. My cum jetted down her throat, and she swallowed every last drop.

Goddamn.

Once she drained every bit of my essence, I pulled her up so she was positioned just over my still fully erect cock. I needed to be inside her now or I might just lose my mind.

The fire was lit and there was only one way to put it out.

I gripped her hips tightly as I thrust up into her. Her sweet moans as she bounced made my head spin. She circled her hips, and I threw my head back and came undone, just barely managing to rub her clit, making her scream out as she joined me in orgasmic bliss.

Needing to be close to her, I pulled her to my chest and wrapped myself around her. I took her in and thought about what this all meant.

Could I do this forever?

"You are a blessing and a curse," I mumbled. She hummed in response.

As much as I didn't want to, I had to go to work and deal with the crisis at hand. I squeezed her ass, and the responding squeak made me chuckle.

"I have to get to work. Cora will ride with Raf to the office and meet you there. Please tell me you will come back from whatever you two will be doing in time for dinner?"

"Of course," she replied as she showered me with kisses all over my chest and neck.

Oh God.

"Good. Now stop that or I will never get to work."

"Oh, but maybe I want that," she said as she looked me in the eyes. Hers were full of lust, and my lion beat against my barriers, wanting to take her, claim her. I pushed him back but smiled seductively as she pouted.

"Later," I commanded as I helped her off the bed.

When she went to stand, she seemed to have sea legs. Her

body took a minute before she could stand on her own, and my chest puffed out, knowing my cock did that to her.

We both got in the shower, and I washed every inch of her perfect body, paying extra attention to certain areas.

When I got to her pussy, I flicked at her clit while I thrust my fingers into her. She collapsed onto my hand, and I pinned her to the wall.

"So damn wet for me, Red," I growled.

She whimpered as I finger fucked her with urgency. This needed to be quick, but I just couldn't resist the temptation. When she cried out and my fingers were caked in her sweet essence, I thought I would collapse and explode with my own release.

"Red, you are going to be the death of me," I growled as I replaced my fingers with my aching, throbbing cock.

"Shit," she moaned as I rammed into her like an animal. Then my lion came forward, and my pace quickened.

"I want to mark our mate," my lion said in my mind as I moved with haste in and out of Red.

My hands moved to her throat, exposing the area of her neck my lion was drawn to. Leaning into her, my lips moved and brushed against the spot.

"No," I growled at my lion and pulled back as we both found our releases.

As she washed me off, I could tell something was off. My lion was pissed and letting me have it.

Fuck me.

"She is our mate. You deserve her just as much as I do. Claim her. Complete the process with your mark."

I ignored him. Part of me knew he was probably right, but I just couldn't. "I…um… took the liberty of getting you an outfit since you, um, don't live on land."

Despite her being upset, she looked at me with an amused expression. I retrieved the outfit from the closet and handed it to her.

When I saw the outfit the other day, all I could think about was Red wearing it, and boy, did she pull it off.

She was a damn knockout.

When we were getting close to the office, I felt Red tense and knew something was wrong immediately. She stopped dead in her tracks, and I turned to ask her what was wrong.

"I-I have to go," she said, then turned on her heels and left. I stood there dumbfounded as I watched her disappear from view.

What the hell? Was this because I didn't mark her? Shit.

My heart shattered, and my lion whined. Just when I thought maybe I could do this, she ran away. Ran away from the monster I was.

DAMN IT!

I stood there paralyzed by devastation. Was she truly gone?

"Where is Aria?" Cora asked, making me jump and break through my haunted thoughts. I shifted my gaze to her, and my shoulders slumped. I felt like I had the weight of the world on me.

"I don't know," I whispered softly.

"Tell me everything," she said.

"We… um… had fun all night and this morning. Then we came here. And out of nowhere, she just… took off."

Cora looked around, then sucked in a breath. She looked me in the eye and said, "Can you deal with whatever you need to do without Raf?"

Umm, okay.

Obviously they had talked about our job at some point. I wasn't sure how Raf would help but I was powerless and desperate so I'd try just about anything.

"Yes."

"I *will* get her back. You just have to trust me."

My head was heavy and my throat tight but I managed to nod. Cora faced Raf. "I need you to explain what you said to me. This company poisoned and killed many of us. Including her father, who is fighting its effects and will soon pass. This is very raw for her."

That got my attention. "I had nothing to do with that accident. I knew something was off about it but can't prove anything. Been fighting the system since."

Cora raised her hands in surrender.

"Easy there," she said. "You know Aria and I are mermaids, right?"

I nodded and she continued. "We have a counterpart called sirens. They are the devil's version of us. Sirens use spelled music to lure ships to their death, which is what happened with your company. Our MerSoldiers tried to stop it, her father leading the interception. But they were too late. We lost so many men, and the ones who lived are slowly dying. One being her father, who is an important man to our kind. Losing him will be devastating if Aria isn't mated. I know you didn't work there at the time, but you are associated with them now. "

As she explained what might have gone wrong and why my mate ran, I felt even more weight come over me. Honestly I had no clue how I was standing. When I felt Cora's hand on my arm, I looked up at her.

"I've got this," she said reassuringly.

I nodded, and she and Raff took off leaving me alone with the weight of the world on my shoulders.

Chapter Fourteen

ARIA

I could feel Cora's presence but it took her a while to find me. When she did, she took a seat next to me, her closeness calming me

"Talk to me, A," she said, breaking the silence.

"There isn't much to say, C. He works for the people responsible for my father and so many others," I sobbed.

"What if I told you he wasn't the bad guy? Yes, he works for the bad guy, but he is doing good."

I looked at her with my eyebrow raised, asking silently what the hell she was talking about. She pointed at Raf.

"Last night when we were getting to know each other, he told me how he worked for an oil company, though not by name, or I would have warned you. He told me how they worked together and were making changes for the good. When we got to the beach this morning, Takar was shattered and confused," she explained. Then waved Raf over. He told me everything as I tried to take it all in.

"I just…I don't know. I mean, obviously we are mates, and

despite not being marked, it is strong. Staying mad at him is not an option. But right now, I just need space. I need time to process all of this in my own way."

"Understandable. Go be with your dad. We will see you soon," Cora said before grabbing Raf's hand and leaving.

Chapter Fifteen

TAKAR

I was at the office and looked up when my door opened. But slumped back when I realized my Aria was not with Cora and Raf.

"Takar, you still have to trust me. She knows the truth, but needs some time to process it all. I know she will be back," she said softly. I nodded, but damn if this shit didn't suck.

"Hey man. I can't imagine your feelings right now, but I do have good news," Raf said. I glanced up. "Did you turn off your phone?"

"Yeah, I needed quiet."

"Well, when he couldn't reach you, he called me."

"Who?"

"Zaz."

Wait, what?

"Zaz!" I exclaimed. "He's…"

"Alive, yes. And he will be home soon from what I could catch. His reception was terrible."

I could only imagine what my facial expression was. My heart was both shattered and happy.

Talk about being torn in all directions.

By making a few phone calls, I confirmed that Zaz was alive and was coming home. To say I was elated was an understatement. But the loss of Red countered it.

Why am I always fucking shit up?

Zaz would know just what to do, and if our past was any indication, he would do everything he could to help. My mind was at war with itself, and I was overwhelmed.

Fuck.

Please get here fast.

Fucking military and their snail's pace. He was alive and I needed him yesterday.

"We need to get her back," my lion said.

"I know. I just don't know how. Relationships aren't something I'm good at," I replied, defeated.

Before everything happened with Red, I hated my job, but now it was a whole new level of hate. In fact, I was getting angry at every little thing. This place hurt Red, and despite what I was trying to do, someone else could do it, because I was done.

When I was alone in my office, I filled out a few applications, then left, heading straight to the bar.

It's been at least a week already, and I was chomping at the bit for Zaz to come home.

I fucking hated this.

My usual bartender smiled when I walked in and gave me a shot of my favorite whiskey. I slammed down the first two glasses, then sipped on the third, running my fingers through my long hair.

"You look like shit."

I jumped at the familiar voice.

Zaz.

Was my mind tricking me?

I twisted my cup, looking at it like it was straight alcohol and not whiskey. A soft chuckle partnered with a smack on the shoulder made my head snap in his direction.

Zaz. Holy shit.

I wasn't expecting to hear from him for at least 30 days, let alone see him.

"Brother," I breathed. He looked tired as hell and like he saw some shit, but he was here, really here. Last I saw, he was under enemy fire, and Lord only knew what happened to him after. He was supposed to be dead, after all. Good news was he appeared to be in one piece. He pulled me into a hug before he took the seat next to mine and ordered us some whiskey.

There was so much I wanted to say and to ask, but he would talk when he was ready. For several minutes we didn't speak, we just enjoyed being near each other again. After a while, Zaz turned to me.

"Let's go somewhere more private," he said as he motioned for the bill. I nodded and headed to the beach. While wandering, I found a secluded spot. It smelled of Red, and I suspected she used it to shift out of sight. I'd spend all my free time here, even sleeping sometimes, just hoping she would come back.

While we walked, he told me what had happened while he was missing. Well, parts he could without violating classified status in some aspects. He went through hell, and I went through my own hell, but mine was mild compared to his.

We sat as the waves crashed into our legs and onto the rocks.

"You look like I feel," he said.

"Ha, you have no idea," I huffed.

"So tell me."

Where do I even start?

I took a deep breath. "Well, I…um… met a girl, but she—"

"Found out you turned into a lion?"

Wait, he knows? How?

My jaw dropped.

"N-no, she found out where I worked. But how did you…"

"Know you were a shifter? You really should stop blocking your lion. When you block him, you block me."

What the fuck?

I was stunned speechless, and I just looked at him like an idiot.

"What do you remember about the attack?" he asked, tapping his hand against his leg.

"Just that you saved me from a lion, but he got in a few scratches first," I replied. He let out an exasperated sigh.

"You were more traumatized than I realized," he mumbled, more for himself, but I still heard it. I cocked my head to the side.

What the fuck is he talking about?

"Takar, you were not attacked by a lion. You were attacked by a group of insurgents. After the mission, you didn't check in, so we searched for you. I found you, but I was too late. They had mortally injured you, and you were bleeding out. My lion shifted, taking control, and once he killed the men, he turned you. Turning you was the only way to save you."

I had no words. All I could do was sit there with my mouth open like I was waiting for a dick to swallow.

"You…" I started, but the words fell short.

"Yes, I also shift into a lion. Now let your lion surface, let me in."

Without even a second thought, I let my walls fall and my lion came forward.

"About damn time, Takar. I was getting ready to riot. It's too crammed in here behind those walls," he growled.

I felt another presence. Zaz and his lion.

"I'm Rebel, Zaz's lion. Have you gotten your name yet?"

Wait, he is supposed to have a name?

Shit, I never asked. I just shut him away.

"I liked it when our mate called me Slash. So my name is Slash."

"So they choose their names?" I asked.

"Yes. I called mine a rebel cause he was being one, and it stuck. But we are not about to look past the girl you spoke about being your mate. Have you claimed her?"

I shook my head in shame and defeat. "I'm a monster. Or at least I felt that way before. Now I don't know how to feel. But none of it matters. I work for the company responsible for hurting her father and killing many of her people. I don't think she will ever forgive me."

"Takar, by now you must realize the mate pull is strong. Just go to her. The rest will work itself out in time."

"I-I can't."

"And why not?" he barked.

"She's a…a mermaid."

A look of shock took over his face. "Oh, that's…um…interesting. Not what I would have ever expected, but the gods work in mysterious ways. Honestly, I would have assumed human but not mermaid."

"I had no clue what was happening. She is the one who told me," I admitted.

"Again, you essentially blocked me out. If I had known, I could have helped you. Hell, you probably wouldn't have even thought of rejecting her because you would have known. But there is nothing we can do about that. Right now, I need you to tell me everything from the beginning."

I told him how I felt a pull to the ocean, how I met Aria and everything since I was turned and the battle within myself.

Over the next several hours, he told me everything he knew, how he was born a shifter and that I was not a monster but a powerful being. He made sure to mention I deserved her, and I needed to find some way to go to her. I resisted, but soon his words started to make sense.

Damn it.

I wasn't broken. I was a powerful protector.

"Okay now, long shot. Do you happen to know any witches?"

"I think so. I mean, not personally, but I may know someone who would."

I called Raf, and he answered right away. "Hey brother, what's up?"

"Um. I need to speak with Cora."

I sighed in relief when he didn't question me and just passed the phone. "Takar, what can I help you with?"

"Do you know a witch who can help me get to Red? I mean Aria."

"Ursa. Yes. I'll text you her address and let her know you are coming," she replied, then my phone buzzed with the address.

"Thanks. I owe you."

"No, you don't owe me anything." She hung up.

The address led us to a small shop, and a woman appeared from the back as we walked in. Her purple hair stood out. Hell, it practically glowed.

"Takar, I knew you would come even before Cora called," she said, then stiffened as her eyes met Zaz, who came in behind me.

Before I could even react, Zaz growled as he pounced over to her, stopping in front of her with no space between them.

"Mate," he snarled. She gasped, then his lips met hers with hunger.

Well, then.

I looked around awkwardly as they continued to practically have sex. I mean he was rock-hard and she wasn't shy about grabbing his protruding cock despite the fact that I was still standing next to her.

"I'm going to devour that sweet cunt right here, right now," Zaz snarled.

Yep, third wheel.

As they moved toward the back, I grew more unsure of what the hell to do.

"Drink the black liquid in the tail-shaped bottle as you enter the ocean. It will give you what you need to go to her," a woman's voice rang in my head.

Deciding not to question it, I looked around for the bottle. Once I spotted it, I grabbed it and took off toward the ocean.

As soon as my feet hit the water, I took it down like a shot. Lights surrounded me, and I held back a scream as my body took on its new form. I knew what was happening since it had happened when I first shifted into a lion.

But damn, this shit hurt.

The lights fell, and I flopped into the ocean with a splash. When I looked down, I gasped at the striking beauty of my black tail. I looked at the bottle again and read the letters etched on the side.

Think Cinderella. Don't turn into a pumpkin.

Okay, so I have until midnight, got it.

I went under fully and looked around. Fuck, where did she live?

As if she knew I would be here and need help, I noticed Cora and Raf waiting further out in the ocean. Without a word, she motioned for me to follow, and I did.

Chapter Sixteen

ARIA

I was so damn confused. There was no denying the mate pull, but he literally worked for the enemy.

I missed Slash so fucking much it was making me sick.

Don't get me wrong, I knew a siren was truly responsible, but I also felt more could have been done by the oil industry to prevent something like this. Obviously, they hadn't known about the lost lives of mermaids, but what about the sea life or Tilly?

Raf explained everything, and how Slash was leading it. Which brought me some peace, but I was still hurting.

Ugh, I hated this.

To pass the time, I visited my dad and did some reef cleaning. I avoided going home for over a week, not wanting to be truly alone. Cora, of course, visited daily despite my sudden mutism.

"Aria," a voice called out, bringing me out of my thoughts. I looked at who was calling my name and saw Kai, my dad's right-hand man. Immediately, I could see the pain in his eyes.

Oh no.

"Your father. He doesn't have much longer," he said solemnly.

My heart dropped and I let out a cry. I knew this day was coming, but I wasn't ready.

Who was ever ready to lose a parent?

My dad was all I had left.

Stupid oil company.

"You have your mate," a voice said in my mind. I pushed it away, not wanting to think about that right now. My dad was more important.

Following Kai to my father's bed, I took deep breaths, trying to stay strong.

As soon as I was at his side, I grabbed his hand. He opened his eyes and smiled weakly.

"My beautiful daughter Aria. Where is your mate?" he asked weakly. My heart clinched.

"He isn't here, Dad," I said, avoiding his knowing eyes.

"Why not?"

Letting out a sigh, I explained everything from the beginning while he listened intently.

"My beautiful daughter, you are just as stubborn as your mother. Did I ever tell you how I met your mom?"

"No," I whispered as I shook my head.

"Before we met, she was dead set on leaving this ocean and going to the coast of Costa Rica. Then she met me, her mate. She refused to accept me but also didn't reject me. It was painful and sickening. I tried everything I could to win her over. Then her mom passed, and she pushed me away even more than before. I gave her space, and she left. But I never gave up. I eventually found her in Costa Rica, and the rest is self-explanatory."

Shit, I had no idea.

My parents grew up here, so I didn't know. As he continued to tell me stories, I could see Slash and me in those roles and my heart ached.

Had I screwed this up?

"Daughter, grieve me but don't let my death stop your happiness. Don't drag this out like your mother did. We lost precious time together. I will always be with you, no matter what."

"Okay, Daddy. I promise," I whispered as he took his last breath.

I clung to him, refusing to let him go despite knowing he was gone. But until I physically let him go, I could feel him.

Now I was alone, an orphan.

Chapter Seventeen

TAKAR

It didn't take long for an underwater city to appear in the distance.

Holy shit.

The buildings were as tall as skyscrapers but made of coral and seaweed. Honestly it reminded me of Seattle but underwater. The colors were somehow more vibrant in the ocean than I could have imagined. This place was gorgeous and part of me didn't want to leave.

As we got close, Cora pointed to a small cottage, and I swam toward it. That's when I saw her holding onto a man who I assumed was her father. I watched as he took his last breath. My heart shattered, breaking completely as she screamed in pain.

No matter what, the people responsible for this would suffer gravely.

"Red," I whispered hoarsely.

Hearing her cry out hurt so damn bad. I wanted to help her, but felt powerless. My lion took control, making me go to her and wrap around her, holding her close. At this moment, nothing else mattered. My presence as her mate could do so much, but I needed her to know I was sorry.

"I'm so sorry, Red, for all of it," I murmured into her ear.

"I'm sorry too. But I am still hurting," she said between sobs.

Right then, it clicked. I had a plan to shut down my company, and since I worked there, I could do it from the inside without a second thought.

"I know, Red. As much as I wish I could, I can't do anything about the past. But I can help you get your revenge on Coil Cove Depot from the inside."

"But you could, no, you would lose your job."

Fuck the job. She was what I lived for. Her worry for me was adorable.

"I'd rather lose my job than lose you," I whispered as I squeezed her closer. She relaxed into my touch and leaned into me. As I struggled a moment for balance, still not used to a tail, she pulled back slightly and looked at me.

"Wait, how are you a mermaid?"

"Cora introduced me to Ursa," I responded. Her eyes shone with gratitude.

"How long until the spell wears off?"

"Midnight."

Before she could respond, a merman appeared and said, "Aria, we are ready to have the ceremony."

Red nodded, and I followed in silence.

The ceremony was beautiful and somehow magical. Instead of a casket, the body was placed on a bed of seaweed. It was surrounded by small fish and was walked down what I could describe as an aisle by crabs. The colors seemed more like those at a wedding, but the mood was not. You could feel the pain in those around you, it was suffocating. The body stopped at the cliff and everyone seemed to come to pay their respects. Then a whale came, honestly can't tell you the kind. A rope of seaweed was attached, and the whale slowly lowered the bed of seaweed into the depths before returning. The whole time I was by Aria's side, providing comfort as she mourned.

Once everyone was gone, I rubbed her back as she cried into my chest, losing myself in my thoughts.

Zaz was right.

I was denying who I was, what I was, and it wasn't just affecting me. Now it was affecting my mate and our bond.

Shit.

I needed to claim her. Not only that, but I think somehow I already loved her.

"Let's get you back to land," she said, bringing me back to reality. Realization of the darkening ocean around me hit me like a ton of bricks.

Fuck.

Chapter Eighteen

TAKAR

She held my hand as we took off toward land. As we got close, I could feel the lights wrap around me. My head broke the surface. The light consumed me and my legs appeared.

After I caught my breath, I stood up and breathed deeply, taking in the salty ocean smell. But that wasn't all I smelled. There was something sweet.

Arousal.

My cock twitched, and Slash came forward freely.

"I want her," he said. I let out a moan when she wrapped herself around me.

"Why didn't you mark me before?" she whispered.

Her question broke my heart. Because I was a coward, an idiot, dead to the world.

The heat radiated from her cheeks against my chest. Was she embarrassed?

Using my fingers, I tilted her face to mine and answered, my voice thick with regret and sadness. "Because I still thought I didn't deserve you."

"And now?"

"I regret not doing it," I said, looking into her eyes. "But I can wait until you are ready."

Oh, how I wanted to take her right here, right now, but she'd just lost her father and it was not the time.

"What if I said I was ready?" Her hands wandered up my chest.

Oh fuck. I hoped she wasn't joking. I didn't think I could handle it.

"I would love nothing more, but don't rush yourself," I hummed huskily. Which definitely told her I wanted her. That and my hard cock poking her belly.

Down boy.

She strained against my hold and brushed her lips against mine. My arms automatically wrapped around her even more. When her legs brushed against my aching cock, I let out a growl at the sensation. My control wavered.

"Careful, if you do that again, I might just fuck you and mark you right here on this beach," I warned.

Slowly, she moved her hand down my body until she got to my aching erection. She grasped it and pulled slightly, making me clench off my orgasm.

In a swift move, I had her on her back beneath me. I looked down at my mate and took in the sight of her. Fuck, she was beautiful, and I wanted to taste her so badly.

I was between her legs, licking her juices in seconds. My eyes rolled at the taste.

Fuck, she was delicious.

It didn't take long for her sweet cum to coat my lips and tongue. That did it.

I made sure to get every last drop she gave me. Then I pushed my length into her. She moaned, and I almost came right there.

No. Not now.

I moved in and out of her, slowly at first, my lion itching to mark her.

Oh, I plan on it.

Without warning, I slammed into her and let Slash come forward a bit. I needed his guidance on what to do, but I had everything else handled.

"Bite her at the base of her neck and hang on for the ride," he said.

I brushed her hair to the side as I leaned in, kissing the sensitive spot before clamping down. As soon as I did, my body shook from the most intense orgasm I ever experienced, and her walls tightened violently around my pulsing cock. I gasped as she bit me in return, giving both our releases a second wind.

Holy shit.

My lion purred in satisfaction.

"Mine," he said.

I moved next to her and pulled her into my chest.

"Land and sea united as one. Power is great. You both shall hear me and each other. You share three forms and have great friends. Act in the ways of Poseidon and you will be rewarded," a deep male voice said in my head.

What the fuck was that?

I looked down at my mate, who was looking at me, her eyes sparking.

"Who the fuck's voice was that?" I breathed.

"Poseidon."

Wait, the god?

I guess I wasn't that surprised. Red was a mermaid, so it made sense.

But why was I hearing him? Not to mention the three forms comment, that one really got me. Like, what the hell did that even mean?

"So many questions. First, I am not a mermaid, so why am I hearing your god?"

"My father had the gift, and his mother before him. Once

mated, the descendent or their mate gets the gift. Though in this case, we both did."

Interesting.

"Okay now, three forms. You don't think you turn into a lion, do you?"

"I don't know, but Ursa might."

Oh, she probably would, but could we get her to leave Zaz alone? I didn't have him blocked, so I knew they were… um… busy.

"About that. She… um… might be a bit tied up." I chuckled at my joke, knowing Zaz was into ropes. So she was probably literally tied to a bed or something random, like a tree. Aria's quizzical look almost made me laugh even harder. "She is apparently mated to Zaz."

I could feel her confusion strengthen through the bond. I brushed my finger on her lips and smiled, a genuine smile. "Lots happened while you were gone. Zaz came back alive. He told me what really happened in Africa and convinced me to go after you instead of letting depression take me."

Her smile melted me. I leaned in for a kiss, which she returned with fire and passion, and I had to stop myself from taking her all over again.

"So when is it safe to visit?"

"Ha, technically anytime, but Zaz has the stamina of a champ, well, lion," I said through laughter. "But I can find out."

I pulled Slash forward. The connection linked instantly, and Rebel responded for Zaz, who was occupied.

"Meet at the beach in one hour."

Figures.

Enough time for ten mate sessions. Horny bastard.

I couldn't blame him one bit, because I was in the same boat.

"We wait at the beach, and they will be there in about an hour," I informed Red. I still had so many questions, but they could wait. She was grieving, and that took priority.

We had forever.

But I couldn't help but wonder if she could turn into a lion.

Chapter Nineteen

ARIA

As I sat between Slash's legs on the beach, he wrapped himself around me and just held me. He finally marked me, and I was in a state of utter bliss. The bond was complete. I turned toward him enough to take in his scent. Frankincense and pine.

He shifted under me and twisted to look behind him. Then leaned down and kissed the top of my head.

"They're here, Red," he whispered against my head.

Reluctantly, I pulled away from Slash's chest and looked to see Ursa with a man, holding hands and smiling.

"Mated as one. Stronger together, shift for land and shift for sea. Together they are of godly power," Ursa said.

Wait, what?

I glanced at Takar. Confusion drew his brows down, and his eyes shone with questions.

"Minds link as one. No need to speak. Your mind is a silent link," she continued.

"Okay, can you speak in something other than these damn

riddles, like seriously," Slash snarked, making me giggle. Ursa rolled her eyes and smiled.

"Basically, you can speak to each other through your minds, and you can shift into a lion and a mermaid. Name's Zaz. You must be Aria." He reached out his hand for me to shake.

I took it and inhaled sharply as he pulled me into a hug. Slash yanked me from Zaz and held me to his chest while he growled possessively.

"Easy brother. You marked her and I'm marked too," Zaz said with his hands up. Slash let out a huff. I placed my hand on his chest, making him relax and look at me.

"So, he can shift into a mermaid, and I can shift into a lion?" I clarified, never breaking eye contact.

"Yes," Ursa said.

"And we can speak through a mindlink?"

"Yes."

"How?" Slash asked.

"You need to concentrate and open your mind," Ursa said.

I closed my eyes and focused on opening up any walls I had, willing the words to flow freely. I gasped when the barriers fell and openness filled my mind.

Holy shit. What should I say?

My mind rushed with possibilities, but my heart screamed "I love you."

Screw it.

"I love you," I mindlinked. He gasped, and I waited for a response.

Soon I felt a tickle in my mind followed by, "I love you too."

My heart fluttered and swelled with joy at those four words. I fought to avoid fucking the man right here. My body was on fire. I opened my eyes, and he was smiling just as broadly as I was.

"Clearly you had some success. So now, the next order of business. You need to let your lions get acquainted. Though not here. Do you have any secluded places?" Ursa said.

Right, lions aren't exactly native to this area so we could not be spotted.

That would be bad.

"I do, but we have to swim there," I said.

Ursa smiled and pulled out two vials for her and Zaz. We headed to the water and walked in until we were waist deep. I shifted, followed by Ursa and Zaz, after they took their potions. Zaz let out a whimper but did well with the shift. I looked to see Slash just standing there.

"Close your eyes and will yourself to shift. Open yourself to the form," I said calmly. He nodded, and I watched as he shifted effortlessly.

Perfect.

I took in the sight, and heat filled my core.

So fucking sexy.

Grabbing his hand, I pulled him further into the water until we were fully underneath the surface. I swam a tight circle around him and checked him out. A lion's head now sat at about knee level, but his tail was still a shimmery black. I brushed my hand over his lion head, making electricity flow between us. His hand touched my tail, and I looked down. I now had a lion's paw on my knees.

It was beautiful.

Slash pulled me to him, and we wrapped our tails together as we embraced.

"So fucking sexy," he whispered into my neck. I moaned as his tail brushed against mine.

"Not now. We'll end up having sex if we continue," I whispered breathlessly.

"Hmmm. Tempting," he murmured against my neck, sending jolts through me.

Oh shit.

Zaz cleared his throat, and I buried my head into Slash's chest. "I'd say get a room, but we need to go."

Now the heat in my cheeks was suffocating. I intertwined our hands, and I led the way to my home, the cave I had made my own. It took Zaz a minute to figure out how to work his tail, but he got it after a few stumbles.

When I looked at Slash, his eyes sparkled with excitement at seeing marine life all around. A dolphin swam alongside him before nuzzling him. He smiled like a kid who had just got the best gift ever. After a while, a sea turtle appeared belly-up below him.

"He wants you to rub his belly," I mindlinked.

He rubbed the turtle's belly like a dog. Sea turtles were essentially the dogs of the ocean, so it was fitting.

As we neared the cave, I slowed down and so did everyone else. I quickly maneuvered through the cave's maze, and we came out on land. Once I shifted, everyone else did, too. Now we had to do some hiking. It wasn't much, but the clearings to let our animals free were not in view of the water.

We broke through the last of the trees and into a beautiful, wide-open clearing.

A safe place to shift.

I found this place one day. My mom used to come here, and now I was going to share it with my mate and our friends.

Slash and Zaz looked around, taking in the lush green grass, the rocky cliffside filled with flowers that had found a way to survive. Honestly, Takar was like one of those flowers, at least to me. The trees stood tall and provided shade, not to mention no one was here, just us.

"This is beautiful," Zaz said, breaking the long silence. I smiled widely.

It truly was.

Chapter Twenty

TAKAR

This shift definitely went better, way less pain. Now that we were in the clearing, my lion practically jumped like a teenager who just saw boobs for the first time.

"Like home," Slash said, completely content. I could hear Rebel snarl in agreement. To say Zaz and I would spend time here was an understatement.

"This is beautiful, " Zaz said.

Took the words right out of my mouth.

"Okay, Takar, you shift first, let Aria see your lion, then I will help her shift," Zaz said, bringing us back to the task we came here for.

"Okay," I said. Zaz was the best fit to answer questions since I had fought this for so long. Not to mention, we had a link that worked in any form. I took a few steps back and let Slash take over.

My paws hit the ground, and I watched her eyes shift. Never once did I see fear, and Slash purred at that realization.

If anything, we saw even more love than before.

My eyes followed her as she moved toward us and ran her hand through my thick black mane. I leaned into her sweet touch, needing more of her.

Fuck, this was heaven.

I watched as Zaz told her what to do. It was easy, since it was similar to shifting to a mermaid.

He told her to watch her distance since she would grow in size and all the good to know stuff. He also warned her it would hurt the first few times. Before I knew it, she was standing before me as a lioness.

A stunning red lioness.

Holy shit.

Her lion introduced herself, already picking her name, Red.

That made me smile since I had given her that name. After a minute, I walked up to her and let Slash take the lead, since all this was new to me.

We rubbed our faces, spreading our scents on each other, essentially marking each other again. I lay down, and she joined me. As we relaxed, I groomed her and nibbled at her ears, making her swat at me a few times.

Zaz shifted, and so did Ursa. Their lions looked identical to each other minus the white spot Ursa had. They too marked each other, then lay down.

"This is heaven," Zaz said to me. I hummed in response.

No, this wasn't heaven. This was something far better.

This was real.

Chapter Twenty-One

TAKAR

I woke up to a sleeping mate curled into my body. We were still in our lion forms, and I enjoyed having my mate asleep against me.

Before now, I never thought I would be at peace with the new me. But Red made everything negative go away. She was my everything and what I lived for.

A buzzing sound made my ears twitch.

What the?

It took me a minute to realize what it was.

My mate and I were purring, well humming.

"Our mate is beautiful," Slash said.

"Yes, yes, she is," I replied. I leaned in and licked her just behind her ear.

She stirred and looked up at me.

"Hey there gorgeous," I linked, my voice thick with my desire for her. She rubbed her face against me, making me purr with pleasure.

"Follow me," she said as she stood up. She stretched and so

did I. Then she pranced over to the woods. I watched her from behind, enjoying the view as I followed. We entered a smaller clearing. It was just as beautiful as the large one, but more isolated.

Suddenly, I was knocked off my paws and rolled against the forest floor. When I stopped, Red had me pinned on my back, looking at me like I was her next meal.

Fuck me.

I growled with lust. "Red, I will take you right here."

"You have to catch me first," she challenged.

Hmm, bet.

In the blink of an eye, I lunged up and flipped her so she was on her back. I nuzzled her neck, making her purr in response.

"Roll over," I ordered. Without wasting any time, she was on her belly beneath me. "Let your lion take over fully."

I felt as she did, and I did the same. It was weird sitting back in the position my lion normally took.

No wonder he was mad at me.

Once done, Slash pulled out and gave me back control, and I felt as if Aria had control as well.

I lay with my paws around her and closed my eyes.

I jumped when a loud ringing filled the air. It didn't take me long to figure out it was my phone. I quickly shifted back to my human form and looked at the caller ID.

"Hey Raf. What's up?" I said into the speaker. Red shifted, and I watched her intently, taking all of her in. She walked up and snuggled into me before kissing my jaw.

Hmm.

"Boss man needs to meet with you later," he said.

Of course he did.

"Okay," I sighed. "I will be there at two on Monday. It's the weekend, and I am currently in the middle of something."

I'll be damned if I was going to end this date now. This was heaven, and honestly, I never wanted it to end. But in order to take down this company, I had to play along for just a little bit longer.

"Sounds good, brother. I'll let him know."

"I want to be with you in my natural form," she whispered seductively as I hung up.

Oh, fuck me.

"Let's go," I growled as I cupped her perfect ass in my hands.

Fuck, she fit so damn perfect.

The excited squeak she let out made my cock twitch in anticipation. I had no idea how sex as a mermaid felt or even worked, but I was excited to find out.

She practically dragged me behind her as we made our way to a small beach on the back part of the island. I watched as she shifted, then shifted myself. It didn't hurt at all.

We swam further into the water, then she was in my arms. I held her close, and our tails automatically twisted together. The muscles in my tail tightened repeatedly against her, creating a magical friction.

Oh fuck.

I let out a moan as electricity flowed through my body, growing with intensity as we moved against each other.

"How does this work?" I managed to say.

My breathing was ragged and my eyes rolled back with the pleasure I was experiencing.

She chuckled against my lips.

"We are doing it," she breathed. "Soon we will orgasm, and my tail will absorb your seed and open up with my orgasm."

As she finished the words, our tails moved more frantically and our kiss grew sloppy. I growled as my body felt like it would explode.

Holy shit.

I had no clue how long I would last. To say I was on the edge was an understatement, and I knew when I fell, I would lose myself in bliss.

Hell, I was already there.

I gripped her hair in a punishing hold as I nibbled at her neck, teasing her mark. "Fuck Red, I think I'm going to…" My words cut off as my body stiffened and jerked from the most intense orgasm I ever experienced. Her scream of pleasure combined with her pulling my hair only seemed to add fuel to my release. Our tails quivered together as we rode out the ecstasy.

When I released her hair, she released mine. Our tails loosened up but still stayed twisted together.

Holy fuck, that was amazing.

Chapter Twenty-Two

ARIA

Now we had been together in every form, and I was in absolute heaven.

My mate had a plan to get revenge for my father and the others lost because of the ship. My mind wandered to a special humpback who was responsible for saving many lives on the day of the accident.

Tilly.

Slash needed to meet Tilly.

She couldn't stop the wreck, but she was able to redirect the ship to decrease the damage. It came at a cost.

If we hadn't saved her, she would have died. Tilly wasn't a god to us by any means, but she was a type of royalty.

"I want to show you something," I said as I separated from him and grabbed his hand before setting off into the depths to find Tilly.

It didn't take long to spot her in the distance. As usual, she sensed us and called out her greeting before diverting toward us.

Her calf, Willy, was right next to her. The confusion was radiating off Takar in waves as he seemed to realize he could understand Tilly.

"We are able to feel what they are saying as mermaids. And they can understand us when we speak," I explained.

"Oh," he said.

"Her name is Tilly and the little guy is Willy." I moved us closer to the pair. "Hey, beautiful, looks like you are doing well with your new little one. This is my mate, Takar, or, as I like to call him, Slash."

Tilly let out another cry, and I noticed Takar's smile.

The tyrant who was Willy bumped his nose to Slash, essentially giving him his approval and trust.

Whales are smart creatures, and much like a dog, they can pinpoint a good or bad person, though dolphins had a stronger sense of this. When Slash petted his head, the little guy squealed.

Dork.

While they had their moment, I checked on Tilly's scar.

Sometimes it would ooze, but today it seemed good. Slash gave me a questioning look before mindlinking me.

"What are you doing?"

"Tilly is special," I replied. "She diverted the boat with her body when the siren lured it to wreck. Tilly made the crash less severe and decreased casualties. While doing it, she was impaled by a piece of the ship. With Ursa's help, we healed her. She is family to us mermaids now, even a bit of royalty."

I could feel him blaming himself again.

That would not do.

"I know I freaked out when I saw what company you worked for, but I know it wasn't you. You didn't cause any of this. Not to mention you are planning on taking him down from the inside, and I will get my revenge that way," I said as reassuringly as possible. Once he nodded, I pulled him under Tilly so he could see her scar.

He brushed his fingers along her scar, then moved to her face. "I will make this right. I promise," he said, looking into her eyes. She cried out her approval, then nudged him, making him spin like a ballerina.

Takar laughed and gave her a quick pat.

Chapter Twenty-Three

TAKAR

I held her hand as we swam a little before heading back to where we left Zaz and Ursa. As we got closer, the realization hit me.

They could be having sex.

I called to Slash to give Rebel a message that we were coming.

Thank God I did, because his reply told me they were in fact getting it on.

Which, I mean, who could blame them?

Not like we were much better. Something about being with your mate was like nothing ever before.

I mean, I wasn't exactly a virgin before I met Aria, but that was nothing compared to being with your mate.

Once in the clearing, I spotted Zaz and Ursa in human form sitting against a tree. I sat by a nearby tree, and Aria settled in right between my legs. Zaz smirked at me, like he knew what we had been doing.

"And in how many different species did you fuck your mate today?" Zaz asked.

I could feel Aria's cheeks heat, and I let out a chuckle.

Typical Zaz, always blunt and dirty minded as hell.

"Wouldn't you like to know, you old perv," I retorted.

We all laughed, then hung out until the sun was beginning to set. Zaz and Ursa needed to get back or they would be stranded. But I truly didn't want this to end.

Being away from the city was peaceful and something the lion in me craved.

My eyes took in the area around us and remembered the clearing from earlier. This would be perfect for a house. Granted, Zaz and I would have to build it. Oh, and maybe Raf too, since no humans could make it here due to the magic.

Red shifted in my arms, and I looked down. I could see the questions in her eyes.

"I can feel that you want something through our bond. What is it?" she asked.

I couldn't help but smile. There was no way to keep secrets from her, not with our bond.

"I was thinking about building a home out here for us. It would be good for our lions."

She smiled ear to ear. "I think we could build three. One in the small clearing and another near my cave, and the last in another small clearing due north. That way, all of our friends can have a place to stay and the big clearing stays open."

I fucking loved this woman.

"I second that," Zaz said. "I need a place to shift openly, and since this is safe from humans, it's perfect. Just let me make a few calls and we can start building tomorrow. Between my mate and Raf, we can get it done in no time."

"I can get some mermen to help as well," Aria said. "We have a boat we can use to transport parts."

"Good, then it's settled," Zaz said with a clap of his hands.

We all nodded. "You two stay. We will head back. Enjoy your night."

We all hugged and said our individual goodbyes, then Aria and I watched as Zaz and Ursa shuffled off to shore.

Just like that, we were alone again.

My eyes raked Red's body, suddenly hungry to be with her again. She pushed me back into the tree, and I lowered myself. She wasted no time straddling me, and my cock twitched eagerly.

"How do you want me?" she breathed into my neck.

Oh fuck.

I brushed my hand down her perfect body as my lips met hers, pulling her into a passionate kiss.

"Like this," I growled, and my cock leaked its pleasure.

Chapter Twenty-Four

ARIA

After spending the whole night making love over and over, we didn't want it to end. But our bodies needed a rest, so we curled together in our lion forms.

"Okay, lovebirds, time to build some shit," Zaz's voice broke through my sleep. As I opened my eyes, I growled my displeasure at being woken up.

When I looked around, I saw supplies everywhere, then noticed Zaz, Ursa, Raf, and Cora.

How the hell?

"I said I have connections in construction and having a witch as a mate made transporting the supplies easy as hell," Zaz said, almost like he sensed my question.

Damn.

"I took the liberty of doing some layouts. Obviously this is your island, so you have final say," Zaz said, holding out a folder. I shifted to my human form and leaned against a still-sleeping Slash.

I didn't blame him. He did work all night, after all.

First, I looked at my friends' places and smiled. They were perfect. The last one was ours. It was everything I could have imagined and more. He clearly had help from my friends. The image I held was my dream house.

My emotions soared, and my heart filled with utter happiness. Slash lifted beneath me. He moved slowly, like he was being careful. Clearly, he could sense I was in my human form.

He nuzzled me as he linked me. "Are you okay?"

I ran my fingers through his mane and showed him the photo. He purred in response.

"Let me shift," he linked. I leaned forward, and he stood before shifting and sitting me between his legs.

"It's perfect," he whispered in my ear. I nodded.

"Alright, let's get started," Zaz bellowed.

I looked up to see several mermen walking up and grabbing tools.

As mermaids, we spent most, to all, of our time underwater. But we built houses underwater, and it was similar to building on land, minus the power tools, that is. Some mermen even have a human education to help with our own world.

"I love you," I said as I kissed Takar.

"I love you too," he said against my lips, then pulled me close. I moaned as I felt his hard cock pressing against me.

"Okay, you two, later. You men have work to do," Cora said as she pulled me away from Takar's embrace. When Takar smacked my ass, a squeak escaped my lips and my cheeks heated.

The guys got to work, and Cora, Ursa, and I went for a walk. We reached the small waterfall and sat on the rocks lining the shore, dipping our feet in the water.

Heaven.

"Hard to believe we all have found our mates so close together," Cora remarked.

"Three best friends with three best friends. Brings a whole new meaning to 'do you have any single friends,'" Ursa said, and we all laughed.

She wasn't wrong, though.

"I'm just glad Takar is finally letting me in," I said. Ursa's face twitched. "Let me guess, trying times to come?"

"Not that I know of, but I know his plan to take down the oil company and industry will be a trial to get through with bumps along the way."

I'll be damned. That was the least riddled thing she has ever said about the future.

"Just be patient. It won't be easy, but the bond you two have is strong and set in stone, having mated in all forms," Ursa added.

I smiled and lay back against the grass, basking in the sun and enjoying the heat. My eyes closed, and I just took in the fresh air.

Chapter Twenty-Five

TAKAR

"You ready to build your home?" Zaz said as he gripped my shoulder.

"Yeah. I can't wait to have a home built just for me and my mate."

The merman named Noah gave us our assignments, and we got to work.

Not only were Zaz and I used to hard work, but we had insane strength, so we were tasked with carrying the large supplies. Ursa had given Zaz a potion to increase his secondary power controlling water enough to dry the foundations quickly. Must be nice being mated to a witch.

Once that was done, the walls started to go up. Partway through the day, a boat arrived carrying insulation. The driver was a mermaid who helped unload and went straight to work. Zaz and I placed all the pieces in the appropriate house area, so everyone had everything they needed right away.

The electrical and plumbing were partially done, and drywall would go up tomorrow. It helped to have a hundred people working. Honestly, we would likely be done in the next few days.

"I'd say we did pretty damn good," Raf said.

"I couldn't agree more," Zaz said.

"I can't wait to be done and um… break it in," I said. We all laughed and headed out to find our mates.

Honestly, it didn't take long. We could sense and smell them easily. When we found them, we all paused at the elegant waterfall in front of us.

Images of me and Red having a picnic, then skinny-dipping under the water filled my mind. Aria was leaning back with her feet in the water, her eyes closed.

So fucking gorgeous.

My cock hardened uncomfortably in my jeans. Her eyes snapped open like she could sense it.

Who am I kidding?

She probably could.

Her stunning eyes met mine, and I couldn't help but smile. "We have to head back to the mainland. I have a plan to set forth tomorrow, and we need to sleep," I muttered.

Tomorrow, my plan to take down the oil company started. I held out my hand to help her up and pulled her to me, wanting the contact.

We took our time walking to the shore to head home. Once in the open ocean, we fell back and just enjoyed the swim to the mainland, since we were not in any rush.

After we made it to my place, Red curled into me, ready to sleep after an eventful day. I kissed the top of her head as she dozed off in my arms.

I would make things right for her one way or another.

Her father's death will mean something.

Chapter Twenty-Six

TAKAR

I was floating on a cloud as I slowly woke.
Hmm.

Pleasure coursed through me and moaning filled the room. As I pushed through my haze, I realized the moaning was me.

What the?

Then I saw Aria's mouth moving up and down my shaft.

Holy shit.

"Fuck Red," I groaned. She hummed against the head of my cock, and I fisted my hand in her hair. "You like it when I fuck that sexy mouth of yours?"

She whimpered, and the smell of her arousal flared. My hips thrust up into her mouth, making her gag. Her responding moan told me she loved it.

"I'm going to cum deep in that sexy throat of yours," I growled as I thrust roughly into her.

"Hmm, yes baby, give me all your cum," she linked, never breaking pattern.

Oh fuck.

My body tensed as my balls drew up. Her teeth grazed my vein, and I exploded.

"FUCK," I yelled out as my orgasm slammed into me. She hummed, sucked, and swallowed until every last drop was spent. "Damn, baby."

She chuckled as she worked her way up my body, leaving a trail of kisses. "I had to give my mate something to think about while he went to work today."

Jesus.

"Oh, I most definitely will be. Even if you hadn't just sucked my dick," I said as I gripped her neck and pulled her to my lips. My tongue pushed at her lips until she parted them, then I dove right in. I could taste my essence on her tongue, and it made me hard all over again.

"Now it's my turn." I spun us so she was on her back and my face was level with her pussy.

Chapter Twenty-Seven

ARIA

His smile was one of a devil who had his prize.

Oh fuck.

He dove down and traced my folds with his tongue. I arched my back in pleasure. His hands moved and pinned me down and dipped his tongue deeper. I moaned and squirmed as he licked and nipped at my bud.

Holy shit.

"Fuck, Red, you taste so damn good. I could live off just your essence," he growled, the vibration sending a shiver down my spine.

My eyes rolled back, and I fought against his pin as he worked my sensitive clit, adding his fingers into my entrance. He hooked his finger and moved in and out.

"Slash," I moaned. I wasn't going to last much longer. I wished we could last longer, but we made up for it in stamina.

Being part lion, we could finish and turn around and go again pretty much without any downtime. Which is what he was banking on because I was about to blow.

"Fuck, baby," I breathed as he added another finger.

"Your pussy is so damn hungry for me. Leaking so damn much," he moaned as his tongue traced my clit, his thumb pressing against my back entrance.

My orgasm lurched to the surface, and I screamed out his name as my body convulsed. He dove in with his tongue as his hand moved to spread my legs. He lapped and sipped every last drop of my release as he moaned.

"So fucking delicious." His tone was filled with fire and unquenchable lust.

Oh Poseidon, help me. He was about to take me hard.

Using his strength, he pulled me onto him so I straddled him. His thick erection teased my entrance. "Hmm, Red, I am going to fuck you nice and hard. Can you handle it?"

"Yes," I breathed. Within seconds, he pulled me down, making me take all of him instantly. "Fuck!"

Oh god, yes.

He wrapped his arms around me and braced them on my shoulders as he pushed me into each thrust. I leaned my head back in pure ecstasy and realized we were standing and not sitting.

Holy shit.

Each thrust sent a jolt through my body as he hit my sweet spot over and over. Our position added sweet friction to my already sensitive clit.

"You like taking my big cock, don't you?"

"Fuck yes."

"Good, cause I will be deep inside you every day, in every form, every chance we have. YOU ARE MINE," he growled.

His possessive tone sent me spiraling over the edge. I screamed as he hit that one spot again, and my muscles tightened almost to the point of pain before numbing pleasure spread over me.

My walls tightened, and Slash growled as his cock pulsed inside me, filling me with his hot seed. He bit down on my mark, making me yell out as I came all over again. I returned the favor and his cum started to leak out of me.

He laid me down and dove back in with his tongue, licking up every last drop of our mixed release. His moans were ones you would hear in a sloppy porno, and they went straight to my crotch, making me want him even more.

"Hmm. My naughty little mermaid wants more of her lion king. Tsk tsk. Well, she will have to wait. I have to get sweet revenge," he purred.

I whimpered as he pulled away. It quickly turned into a moan when his lips met mine, giving me a taste of us.

Oh Poseidon, it was sinful.

Taking my mate would never get old. He was so damn sinful, and I loved every second of it.

"Lion king, huh?" I mused.

He chuckled deeply. "Well, it is accurate."

"True. Maybe I will call you my King now," I teased as I twisted my fingers in his messy hair. I felt his cock twitch, clearly liking the sound of that.

Good to know.

"Maybe I will call you my Maid since you do so damn good serving my starving cock."

Oh fuck.

"Hmm, I will always be at your service, my mate, my King."

His lips slammed into mine as he grasped the back of my neck punishingly.

"Mmm, yes please," I hissed. "Handle me, King."

I never would have thought I'd be into rough treatment or even this dynamic, but here I was leaking copious amounts of desire onto my now-dripping thighs. Takar's nostrils flared and his eyes shifted.

"On your knees. Your King needs to cum in that sexy little mouth of yours again."

Fuck me.

Chapter Twenty-Eight

TAKAR

Seeing my mate on her knees eagerly taking my cock down her heavenly throat was a sight I would never tire of. Her seductive moans vibrated straight to my balls, and I knew I wouldn't last.

She was too damn skilled with that tongue of hers.

I gripped her hair roughly as I slammed my length in and out of her sinful mouth. Her hands cupped my balls, and I stumbled back. Luckily, I ran into a hard surface, so I didn't fall. She never missed a beat. I was in sensory overload, and my throat couldn't muster coherent words.

"Is my Maid going to take her King's load like a good girl?" I linked, still unable to speak out loud.

"Yes, my King," she linked back. Her tone was filled with desire, and I came undone.

My knees buckled from the force as jet after jet of my cum sprayed into her mouth. She slurped and swallowed every drop until I had nothing left to give.

She released my sated cock with a pop, and I helped her up, pulling her to my chest.

"So fucking perfect," I whispered against her lips.

My tongue moved across her lips, seeking a taste of my release in her mouth. She opened willingly, and my cum mixed with her taste was intoxicating.

After a few minutes, I reluctantly pulled away. "Fuck, Red. I want so much more, but your King has a meeting and a company to take down. Meet me at the beach later so we can return to our home. Slash wants time with his Red."

"Hmm. Yes. We will be there."

"Good. I love you."

"I love you too."

With one last kiss, I turned and headed to the office.

To say concentrating on work was hard was a damn understatement. All I wanted was to be with my mate. I was learning so much about her so quickly. Fantasies that I had that I thought she would never be into were, in fact, her desires, too.

How did I get so damn lucky?

The way I treated her at first was deplorable, embarrassing even. But she took it all in stride, and now she was truly mine.

"Takar. I need you to get your damn head out of the clouds," my annoying boss snarled.

I resisted the urge to roll my eyes. Then had to bite my tongue so as not to tell him to fuck off. The man has always been a pain in the ass, and very unlikable. But with what I now knew, my hatred for him was all-consuming.

I closed my eyes and took a deep breath, trying to calm myself. This wasn't the right time, and I was not about to expose my plan.

"Right. What seems to be the issue with the budget?" I refused to apologize to the man.

"Spending is up. Takar, I thought I told you to make all cuts. I don't give a damn about regulations," he yelled. I gritted my teeth.

No, all you care about is your pocketbook.

"Boss. You know the fines and legal trouble could put you in prison, right? This is not something I am comfortable doing. I can get the legal minimum, but that is all."

"Maybe I will just find someone else to do the job."

"Have you looked outside? People are about to riot. No one is going to want to come into shark-infested waters already looking for blood. You are stuck with me, and I am telling you no."

He didn't speak another word, just stormed out of my office and slammed the door. I got up and locked it before pulling out my recorder and hitting stop. Raf had told some protesters about the corruption in the company, and they were sitting outside ready to do some damage.

I looked out my window and saw a friend, Simon. He was a good guy and served with me, Zaz, and Raf. Raf said he was coming to the area, and he volunteered to help with the plan. He was the leader of the protesters, and we were the ones calling the shots from the inside.

Every day, more and more people would show until we made the call. That and the evidence I was collecting as my boss got into hot water would ruin him. Until then, I would continue to do what I do best.

Playing the system.

After tons of paperwork and a hundred or so emails, it was quitting time. I couldn't get out of there fast enough. Not only did I need my mate, but we needed to check on the progress of our home.

As I busted through the doors to the beautiful outdoors, Raf called out from behind me. I turned to him, and he smiled.

"You going to the island?"

"Yep," I said.

"Cora and I will join you. We were planning to check on the construction and all."

"Of course, man. I am meeting Aria at the beach."

"Well, she is probably with Cora, so I guess we can head that way."

With a quick nod, we both headed to the beach.

Chapter Twenty-Nine

ARIA

As soon as Takar left, I called Cora. "Hey, you down to hang?"

"Um, duh. What the hell kind of question is that?"

She truly sounded offended. I let out a chuckle. "Okay, silly question. Want to meet at the bakery on the strip?"

"Yeah, be there in fifteen."

I called Ursa next. "Hey, meet me and Cora at the bakery."

"Sounds like a plan," she replied, then hung up.

Raf and Takar were working today, and Zaz was managing the construction on the island, so us girls were going to shop.

We would need furniture and clothes, after all.

I arrived first and found us a table in the back. Most people wanted the view, so when we came here we took the back so people would be less likely to hear something they shouldn't. Shifters of all kinds were secretive. It was an unspoken rule.

Don't expose yourself.

Cora walked in and headed straight to our usual table. She wore mated well. Her happiness was practically oozing from her

107

pores. Ursa joined us, and the waitress brought our usual. We always got the same thing. A half dozen donuts, three maple bars with sprinkles, and the caramel apple fritters. Then three white chocolate caramel white coffees. Honestly, white coffee was the best, in my opinion. The purest form of the coffee bean, a strong nutty taste with maximum caffeine.

"What are you going to do with your place here? Sell?" I asked Ursa before taking a bite of my first donut.

"Turn it into a shop with living quarters just in case," she replied before taking a sip of her drink.

"That sounds like it would be a dream come true. A chance for you to serve the community," Cora said after swallowing her bite.

"Exactly," Ursa said.

After we finished, we headed to the mini-mall on the beach. Honestly, it was a clever placement. Most stores catered to the beach, but there were plenty of everyday stores mixed in. My favorite was Maurices.

We spent hundreds on new clothes to tease and impress our mates, then headed inland a bit to get furniture. Our last stop was a department store to get appliances. We arranged for it to be brought to Raf and Takar's place so we could transfer it via a spell.

Now it was time to head back to the beach and wait for our men.

Well, mine and Cora's since Zaz was already on the island.

<h1 style="text-align:center">Chapter Thirty</h1>

TAKAR

Raf and I discussed our plans and sent a text with the rundown to Simon. As we got close, we heard the girls laughing and having a good time.

"You ladies having fun without us?" I asked as we got within earshot.

In the blink of an eye, Red was in my arms. I chuckled as I stepped back so I wouldn't fall over.

"I missed you too, Maid," I whispered. My nostrils flared when her sweet arousal made it to my nose. "Hmm, already hungry for my dick, I see."

"Starving," she breathed while nipping at my ear.

Oh fuck.

"Well, let's get home, shall we?"

We all entered the water and shifted. Ursa swallowed her potion. It didn't take us long to get to the island and shift back. We made it to the big clearing and saw Zaz sitting with some of the mermen.

Ursa was at his side in seconds, and he kissed her deeply in greeting.

"How did today go, Zaz?" I asked, essentially breaking their kiss. I heard a snarl of annoyance, but he looked at me and smiled.

"Well, we all have homes now. Just need furniture. Which, if I'm not mistaken, will be here tomorrow?"

"Yes," Ursa said.

"So tonight Raf and Cora will have to sleep in her ocean home."

"Sounds fair."

I wished Raf could shift into a lion. He was just human and now a mermaid, but it wasn't the same.

"Zaz," I linked only to him.

"Yes?" he replied.

"Is it possible to turn him into a lion?"

"Technically yes. But that is his choice, not ours. It would also affect Cora."

"Before we go to our homes, Raf, can we speak to you and your mate?" Zaz asked.

"Sure, man."

Aria and Ursela checked the houses while we headed to the waterfall.

"What's up, man?"

"Takar had an idea, and it affects both of you. So we need to talk to both of you about it," Zaz said.

"Alright, shoot," he replied.

"You now know the story of how I saved Takar."

"Yes," they both said.

"You also now have a mate who gave you the ability to shift into a mermaid."

"Yes," Raf said.

"Everyone in our group can turn into a lion except the two of you. How would you feel about changing that?"

"You mean you want to turn us?" Cora asked.

"Essentially, yes."

"But only if you both want to," I added.

"I only have to turn one of you. Unlike Takar, you won't be scarred since your lion would be allowed to heal you fully. Then the next time you mate, whoever I turn will mark you again, and you will gain the ability at that point."

Cora and Raf looked at each other and seemed to speak with just their eyes. Mermaids don't have a link ability like lions, so this was unique to them.

"Turn me," Raf said, and Cora smiled.

"Raf, it will hurt. More than shifting into a mermaid since you are also growing in size and over your full body, not just part. Granted, it will only hurt the first few times, but when I turn you, you will feel as if you are on fire for several minutes. I need you to know this before I turn you. Takar never got the choice due to urgency, but this is different."

"I understand," Raf said. Zaz turned to Cora.

"It will also hurt for you as well, minus my bite and claws."

"I understand," she said.

"Okay. I will shift and turn you, Raf. Then you stay here and mate. Once you are done, join us in your lion forms."

They both nodded, and Zaz shifted into his black lion. He walked up to Raf and stood directly in front of him, towering over him easily.

"Tell him to turn around," he linked.

"Raf, turn your back to him," I said. Without a word, Raf did what I directed. Cora stood next to me since the first shift was uncontrolled and we didn't want her getting hurt. Zaz lifted his paw and swiped across Raf's back, making him cry out.

Next, Zaz bit down on his shoulder and stepped back as Raf began to shift. Aria's worry flowed through the bond. I linked Red to tell her everything was alright and I would explain later. It was clear she had heard Raf's scream.

In seconds, a majestic lion was standing before me and Zaz. I shifted and found that we could now communicate.

"As your creator, I am your Alpha, but I will not control you or direct you. You are your own leader. But we are linked in all forms. Now shift," Zaz ordered Raf. That was the only way to shift back.

He was human again in seconds. No scars covered his back, just like Zaz said. Cora was in his arms in seconds, and Zaz and I headed back to our mates.

Chapter Thirty-One

ARIA

"Hey Aria," Finly said.

"Hey man. How have you been?"

Finly was a friend. We weren't as close as I was to Cora, but he was still a close friend. We nicknamed him Flou, short for Flounder. With my dad being sick and the pull to land, I had neglected my friends. Cora not as much, but she was also my dad's caretaker.

"I've been doing better," I said.

"I'm glad. I'm so sorry about your dad," he said solemnly.

"Thanks, Flou."

A scream filled the air. Not just any scream, but one of pain. Ursa and I looked at each other.

What the hell?

I relaxed a bit when Slash told me everything was okay. Even before he said it, I knew he would explain. Ursa was clearly also linked by her mate, since she relaxed too. It wasn't long before I could feel Takar approaching. His arms wrapped around me and pulled me to his chest. I automatically leaned into the motion.

"So why the scream?" I asked.

He hummed against my neck. "Raf is now a lion and is currently mating with Cora."

I gasped and turned to face him. "Really?"

"Yes, my Maid. Your friend will soon be running with you."

My smile spread across my lips, and I had to stop myself from jumping up and down.

"I'm assuming she agreed to this," Ursa said.

"Yes, I informed her myself. Her and Raf talked, well, spoke with their damn eyes, creepily. But long story short, they consented," Zaz said.

"So…how long do you think until we see them?" Ursa teased. We all laughed.

"Probably in the middle of the night," Zaz replied.

"Well, lions are horny as fuck," I said.

"Ten times in an hour," Takar added.

"Ha. That's a good one," Zaz laughed.

"I mean, it's true," Takar said.

"Yes, very," Ursa said in a seductive tone. I hummed my agreement.

My stomach growled, and Takar looked down at me. "Sounds like my Maid is hungry for something other than my cock."

My cheeks heated as I buried my face in his chest. He chuckled as he put his fingers under my chin and tilted it up. His eyes shifted color for a second, and I knew Slash was present.

"Don't hide those pretty red cheeks from me or I might have to make your other cheeks just as red later."

Oh Poseidon, have mercy.

I clenched my thighs as liquid pooled between them. He smirked knowingly. "Oh, does my Maid like the sound of that?"

"Yes," I breathed.

He leaned down and brushed his lips against mine. "Good to know."

Fuck me.

Chapter Thirty-Two

TAKAR

I was beginning to enjoy this King, Maid dynamic and teasing her.

Fuck, I would do anything to make this woman happy. If she had a fantasy or a kink, I would put my feelings aside and give it to her. Though it seemed we both had the same ones so I doubt I would have to.

"As much as I want to take you right here, right now, you need to eat first."

As if right on cue, a few mermen appeared with trays of food. Before I was turned into a lion, I hated fish of all varieties. But since I turned, I loved fish to the point I needed to have it daily.

From what Zaz said, it's somewhat a lion thing, but it's mostly a mate thing. He likes fish, but his mate is a witch, so his is a normal craving for salmon and freshwater fish, not sea fish or sushi like me.

Yet another thing drawing me to my mate, I guess.

We all enjoyed our food and sat with each other, talking. I

made sure some food was set aside for Cora and Raf. They would for sure be hungry after mating.

"Miss Aria, the MerKing would like to see you tomorrow," a merman said. His hair was blue, and he wore a yellow tracksuit.

"Of course. Does he request my mate as well, Flou?"

"Yes," he said, bowing his head.

"Do you work tomorrow?"

"Yes, in the morning. I can be off by noon if me and Raf leave here early," I replied, and Red nodded.

"I will let the MerKing know."

"Thank you," she said.

Once it was just me, Red, Zaz, and Ursa, I looked at my mate. "Red, what do you think the MerKing wants?"

She took a deep breath. "Well, my father passed and word has likely gotten to him that I am mated. Which means the ability to connect with Poseidon has been given to one of us. Though somehow we both got it. He probably needs a reading. Plus, give his condolences and congratulations."

"Hmm, that makes sense."

The sound of a twig snapping made all of us look over in the direction it came from. I smiled broadly when I saw two lions coming toward us. The four of us stood and shifted into our lions and got acquainted. Cora's lion likes being called Layla, and Raf likes Ramon. I also found out Ursa's likes being called Sabrina.

We all lay down with our mates and enjoyed the quiet.

"Let's go to our home. I need to ravish you," I linked to Red. She lifted her head and looked at me. Her own hunger sparkled in her eyes. As if we were the flag drop in a race, everyone was up and heading to their homes for the night.

I knew we would be sleeping outside in our lion forms, but there were plenty of walls and counters to use as props.

Once at the little cabin, I shifted and so did Aria. Before she could even take in the progress they made, I had her slammed into the wall.

"Maid, your ass is mine tonight," I growled in her ear as I cupped and kneaded her perfect cheeks, getting me a whimper. "You will wear my handprints and feel my cock all day tomorrow."

Her knees buckled as her body shook, her scent flaring with her arousal.

Fuck. How the hell did I get so damn lucky?

"Don't worry, Maid. I will make you soar to the skies."

"Mmm," she said.

I grasped her hair and pulled her inside before pushing her to the counter in the kitchen. I yanked her hair until she was bent over in front of me. In a swift movement, I had her pants dropped to the ground, exposing her perfect ass.

I licked my lips, knowing I was about to be deep inside her tight ass. But first I wanted a taste. She squirmed against my hold, and I couldn't help but laugh.

"Feisty, are we?" I teased. Then dove to lick up her crease until my tongue teased her perfect hole.

So damn delicious.

Every tease of my tongue caused her to quiver and moan under me. My free hand reached under her and teased her leaking pussy.

Oh, she is most definitely hungry for my cock.

I worked my tongue in her hole while my fingers worked her clit. My grip on her hair was unforgiving. She moaned and rocked against me, begging for more.

"Hmm, such a slut for me, Maid," I growled, then released her hair to slap my hand hard on her ass.

"Oh," she yelled as her body shook.

I kneaded the mark I had left, then moved up to give it a soft kiss. Without warning, I did it again and again. Based on how red she was, she was going to be sporting some bruises.

Fuck. More marks of our love.

My finger worked faster and harder on her clit while my other hand began to manipulate her hole. We didn't have lube, so

I would stretch her as much as I could, then use her cum as our lube.

"King, I'm going to cum," she cried out.

"Yes, Maid, cum for your King," I snarled as I quickly removed my hand from her ass and my pants from my legs.

In an instant, she screamed out my name and her sweet release coated my fingers. I scooped every drop from her, then rubbed it over my length and around her hole.

"Are you ready for my cock, Maid?"

"Y-yes," she moaned. I pressed my tip against her and pushed in just enough to get past the first layer of resistance. She tensed beneath me, and I gripped her hips, fighting the urge to dive all the way in.

"Relax, breathe," I instructed.

As soon as she relaxed, I moved in a little more until I was flush against her ass. "Fuck, Red. So damn tight."

My head spun from pleasure, and I had no clue how long I would last. Lions in general didn't last long. But this had me seeing stars already.

"Fucking punish me, my King," she purred.

My cock hardened more than I thought possible at her command to be punished.

"Make me wear your bruises," she begged.

Oh hell.

I pulled back to the tip, then slammed into her and gripped her hips roughly. Leaning down, I bit her up and down her back as I smacked her ass over and over with every thrust. Her yells and moans let me know just how much she liked it.

My free hand reached down and worked her clit, and she all but melted onto the counter. My movements were erratic and rough. Her ass was now the color of her hair. My balls drew up, and I was about to blow.

I yanked her hair, bending her upper half off the counter as I continued to slam into her. Nipping at her ear, I heard her breath hitch.

"Cum now," I commanded as I slammed into her.

I roared and jerked hard as my orgasm barreled to the surface, her walls tightening around my pulsing length as she screamed out her own pleasure.

Holy shit. I was dizzy from the intense release and had to grip the counter to not fall over.

"Shit, Red, you knocked me on my ass with yours."

She chuckled and wiggled herself, making my cock slip from her heat. Then she was facing me.

"Glad to be of service," she hummed.

Oh. My. God.

Chapter Thirty-Three

ARIA

The way Slash took my ass was blissfully painful. He was quite a bit larger than me, but fuck if I didn't like his rough handling. I could feel the bruises but also knew as soon as I shifted, they would be gone.

Which also meant he could hurt me all he wanted and no one would ever know. As much as I wanted more of him, we both needed sleep. Tomorrow we had a meeting with the MerKing.

RAF AND TAKAR went to the mainland while Zaz, Cora, Ursa, and I stayed behind. The furniture arrived, so we were fast at work arranging everything. Flou was helping me along with Bash, my cousin. It was fun to see them in their mermaid form. Bash sported red hair to match his red tail. Flou had bright blue hair and a yellow tail.

We all sat on the beach, waiting for Takar and Raf to return. When I heard ruffling, I turned and smiled as my mate walked toward me. Clear hunger filled his eyes. He reached out to me and I took his hand, then was yanked up into his chest.

"How was your day, Red?" he whispered against my lips.

"Good. Our house is done."

"Hmm. We will just have to break it in some more tonight. I don't work the rest of the week, so that sexy, hungry ass and thirsty pussy are mine later."

Oh fuck.

"Now let's go see your MerKing."

"See you all later, don't wait up," I said.

Who knew how long we would be?

The MerKing was a talker and was like a second dad to me.

Once in the water, we shifted, and I led the way to the palace. The guard bowed to us as we entered the castle grounds.

Odd. I don't remember my father being bowed to. Respected, yes, but not like this.

When MerKing Titan came into view, he smiled from ear to ear. "Aria, my child. Thank you for coming and bringing your mate."

"Of course, Your Majesty," I said as I bowed. Takar followed my lead.

"Enough formalities. We have business to discuss. Please have a seat," he said, motioning to the vast table before him. We took our seats and looked to the MerKing to continue. "As you know, I do not have a child, and as MerKing, I need to find a ruler for the sea."

I didn't answer so as not to interrupt, but I nodded.

"Your father was able to speak to our god, and I helped raise you after the accident."

As he spoke about the tragedy, I felt Takar stiffen next to me. I rubbed his back and felt him relax.

"I also know the prophecies of your union with your mate. I may not have had a mate who lived long enough to give me a child, but the god Poseidon did give me you through your father," he said proudly.

My eyes began to water. Yes, mermaids could cry.

"The council has voted. Aria, descendent of Cove, head guard of the Righteous Reef. You are now Her Majesty the MerQueen, and your mate Takar Tahaton will be MerKing."

I could feel the shock coming from my mate, and I had to admit my mind was spinning. Not only did the MerKing want us to take over, but he had already brought it to the council.

"I know Takar is working to take down the company responsible for the devastation that cost many lives. This will take him away from the home of the sea, but my darling Aria, I have trained you your whole life for this role without you ever knowing. You were always going to be the MerQueen."

"Your Majesty, I—"

"Please, you are my equal now. Call me Titan. This time tomorrow, you will be formally crowned, and I will take my place on the council as your advisor. Then I shall call you Your Majesty the MerQueen."

Holy shit.

"My King and Queen will bring wealth to Merkind. Wealth to the pride among them, and justice to many," Poseidon's voice said. I snapped my head over to look at Takar, who wore the same confused and excited expression.

Did that mean he was to lead the Lions too?

What would that make Zaz?

"King of land and sea, armed with a warrior on each and the magic within," Poseidon continued.

So Zaz was his warrior with Ursa. But who was mine?

My mind flashed with memories of Flou and Bash always making sure no one messed with me in school or anywhere for that matter.

Okay, so it was settled. Flou and Bash would be my warriors. And bonus Cora was also a skilled fighter and, as MerQueen, I needed more guards. Poseidon confirmed the realization in my mind.

I am going to be MerQueen.

Unbelievable.

Chapter Thirty-Four

TAKAR

My mind was spinning, unsure how to process everything that had just happened. I was to be MerKing and, not only that, but the Pride Male. I had no words, so I stayed quiet. When the MerKing left, I just blinked.

Is this even real?

"Slash," Aria whispered in my ear. I snapped out of my haze and turned to her. Her eyes sparkled in wonder, but as she looked me up and down, her eyes filled with hunger. "Let's go home."

Obviously, we needed to tell the others, but for now, she needed me.

"How do you want me?" I purred into her neck.

"Like this," she said as she pulled me toward the cave.

Hmm.

Once we were under where our house sat, her tail wrapped around mine and we rubbed against each other, creating intoxicating friction. I could never last in this form. From the information I have managed to gather, it is quick, since predators lurk in the shadows of the sea.

I felt myself getting close, and I claimed her lips with mine. She moaned and let me in. We tasted each other as our tails moved.

"Fuck," I cried out. "Red, I'm about to—"

I couldn't even finish the sentence before I came undone. Red's scream only added fuel to my orgasm.

"Hmm, fuck Red, so damn good," I said as I came down from my release.

"Guh, I need more of you so damn bad, but we have a pride to inform," she said breathlessly. I groaned and reluctantly pulled away.

"Let's make this quick so I can fuck my queen," I whispered as I flicked my tongue on her ear.

She whimpered before grabbing my hand and headed toward land.

The sooner we did this, the sooner I could be balls deep in my mate.

I linked Zaz and told him to gather everyone in the big clearing. When we arrived, everyone looked at us with curious expressions.

How would Zaz take that I was his leader now?

Only one way to find out.

$$\text{Chapter Thirty-Five}$$

TAKAR

"As most, if not all of you know, my father had the ability to speak to the god Poseidon. When he passed, it was to transfer to me or my mate. In our case, we both gained the ability," Aria said. Cora and Raf nodded, and Zaz seemed impressed, while Ursa smirked like she knew something.

Interesting.

"Also, as you know, my father passed away from the effects of oil poisoning. My dad was sick and unable to care for me at times, so the MerKing helped raise me. What you may not know is that his mate passed before giving him a child to inherit his throne. He has deemed with the vote of our council that I am to be MerQueen and Takar MerKing."

Cora jumped up and clapped her hands in excitement. "I would love to have you as my MerQueen."

"And I want you to be my right hand. Bash and Flou, you are to be my guards."

"I accept," Cora said before slamming into Aria, nearly

knocking her over. I moved, so she fell against my chest, and laughed at the pair.

"Poseidon spoke to us as well," I added, knowing it was my turn. "I am to be Pride Male on land."

I glanced at Zaz. He was the one I needed approval from since he was my creator and had been my boss since the day we met. He smiled and stepped toward me, stopping just in front of me.

"I will follow you and your commands. Rebel and I accept you as our Pride Male and will obey you and serve you how you see fit," he said, looking me in the eyes. I could see the sincerity in his words through his eyes.

"You also need an advisor," Cora said.

Well, damn. Why didn't I think of that?

"Zaz, will you be my advisor?"

"I'd be honored."

I turned to Raf. "Will you be my guard?"

"Of course, brother."

"You need another guard, Takar," Ursa said. "The gods speak. He is human now, a brother who is mated to one of the MerQueen's men."

"He?" I asked.

"Yes, a merman and a male lion."

Hot damn. Wait. Could it be?

"Simon," I whispered. Ursa nodded.

Holy shit.

"He knows nothing of this life. We would have to tell him everything," I said, looking at Zaz and Raf. "I will need your help with this one."

"Of course," they both said.

"We will meet with him tomorrow," I said. Everyone nodded their agreement. "Now let's shift and enjoy the evening."

With that, we all shifted. Red looked at me. "The only guard I have who is gay is Flou," she linked.

"Well, that could be an interesting pair," I replied.

"Agreed."

Chapter Thirty-Six

ARIA

All of us let our lions forward and played around, just enjoying the bliss we were creating. After several hours, we headed to our new homes to get some much-needed rest. I was curious if Flou and Simon would be mates and how they would react together.

I was leaving the informing to Takar since Simon was his friend. While he did that in the morning, I would meet with the MerKing and iron out details. The hope was to have Simon there, but we had no clue if it would work out that way.

Once in front of our place, we shifted to our human forms, and Takar scooped me up. I clung to his neck, giggling, and he carried me inside.

He moved with haste through the house until we were in our room. I flew as he tossed me onto the bed, then stalked over me like I was his prey.

My core heated as his hungry eyes raked up and down my body while he licked his lips.

Oh fuck.

"My Maid, my Queen, your King wants to have his dessert," he growled.

"Then eat me, my King," I moaned.

Within seconds, I was naked and so was he. He stood back, eyefucking me while he lazily stroked his hard cock. I couldn't help but lick my own lips. He wasn't the only one wanting a taste.

The growl my mate let out almost had me cumming right then.

Oh Poseidon.

He positioned his face at my pussy and his cock just above my mouth.

I teased his tip with my tongue, resulting in a deep moan. His tongue lapped between my folds before devouring my clit. He nipped at my clit and I lurched up, making me gag against his cock deep in my throat.

"Hmm, yes, choke on my cock, Maid," he growled.

Why was that so damn hot?

Tears streamed down my face as I gagged again and again on his length. Each time, he would nip at my bud and thrust his fingers into my core. I knew I wouldn't last much longer. I cupped his balls in my palm and manipulated them while grazing my teeth along his vein.

"Fuck," he cried out as his warm cum filled my mouth. I sucked and swallowed every last drop.

He thrust his fingers faster and his tongue worked harder. My body numbed, and I knew I was about to fly.

His hum vibrated my clit in all the right ways, and my body came slamming down. Pleasure soared as I twitched and convulsed with the force of my orgasm. He worked to get all of my essence.

He collapsed onto the bed and flopped onto his back. I took a minute to catch my jagged breath.

That was intense. Though every time with us was intense.

I climbed onto his broad chest, straddling him. His hands

automatically moved to my hips. He opened his eyes and looked over my body. He moaned.

"So damn beautiful," he growled.

I ground my hips and let out a moan of ecstasy as I felt his hard cock poke me. Slowly, I moved to position myself when we heard our front door swing open.

What the?

Takar was up and in his shorts in seconds.

"Wait here," he ordered, then left.

Chapter Thirty-Seven

TAKAR

I crept through the house to see who had just barged in without knocking.

I swear this better be a damn emergency.

When I rounded the corner, I was definitely not prepared for what I saw. A human.

Simon.

How the fuck?

Not only that, but he was bleeding and looked dead. I couldn't tell if he was breathing and that scared me.

Before I could react, Ursa and Zaz came into view. I looked at them for answers.

"As a witch, the gods speak to me. Simon was under attack and about to be killed. I used my powers and transported him here. Unfortunately, the damage is done. He must be turned in the next few minutes or he will die," Ursa said, her voice calm but full of urgency.

I looked at Zaz, who nodded. "My lion senses it, death. But you are Pride Male, so it should be you who turns him."

"H-how?"

"Just as I did with Raf and you. Scratch his back, then bite him before ordering him to shift."

I didn't respond. Instead, I just nodded as he stepped back.

"I will guide you," Rebel said in my mind.

My heart ached. This was not how I wanted to do this. But he was my brother-in-arms and I was not about to let him die. I only hoped he would forgive me.

We moved outside, and Red came up behind me as I shifted. Slash filled her in through the link while Zaz held Simon up, so I had the access I needed. I was nervous, but my lion and Rebel calmed me.

I lifted my paw and clawed his back before biting him on the shoulder.

"Shift," I snarled through my mind and watched as the man before me turned into a lion.

"Have him stay a lion and heal. It will only take a few minutes," Zaz said. I looked down at him as he slept.

I really hoped he would be okay.

After several long minutes, he began to move. His eyes widened as he realized he was not human. I could feel his panic.

"Easy, brother, you are okay," I linked to him.

He shook his head violently. "Takar?"

"Yes, Zaz is here too," I replied. He looked around and saw Zaz, who was now also in his lion form. "We will explain it all. Shift."

He shifted back to his human form as the rest of us did. "What the fuck happened?"

"You were attacked. Whoever they were, they were killing you. Ursa is a witch, and she transported you here. There is a prophecy attached to you, so the gods intervened."

Zaz stepped in and explained how he was born this way, but he'd turned me to save me, then Raf chose this after meeting his mate. Basically, the whole rundown including my and my mate's status. Then Ursa told him about the prophecy.

"So I am your guard?" he asked, looking at me.

"Yes," I replied.

"But you also shift into a mermaid, so wouldn't I need the ability as well?"

"Yes, that is where your mate will come in. We believe we know who it is," Aria said. "I have called for him. He will be here soon."

"We will need a house built for them," Red linked.

"I will get Zaz on it," I replied.

Simon continued to ask questions while we sat in the living room. Raf and Cora joined us. We told him everything about taking down the oil company and the true reasons why. He was even more on board than before. Zaz promised he would find out who attacked him so we could provide justice to our world.

There was a knock on the door, and all eyes were on Simon. Aria got up to get the door and embraced her friend before letting him in. As soon as Flou and Simon's eyes met, the house almost seemed to shake at the intensity of their connection.

"Mate," they both said simultaneously.

In seconds, Flou had Simon's hand in his, and they disappeared into the woods. Everyone just looked at each other, dumbfounded.

"Well, we know the woods and ocean aren't safe tonight," Zaz remarked, and we all laughed.

"As long as they go to the coronation, I couldn't care less," I said.

"Agreed," Aria said.

"Well, I will leave you two be, since we, um, interrupted you," Zaz said, and I rolled my eyes. "But we will discuss a house location for the pair, and Bash will need one, too. Hopefully, we will find his mate soon."

With that, everyone left. I smirked at Aria. "Now where were we?"

Chapter Thirty-Eight

ARIA

I swung my legs over so I was straddling him, his erection already making itself known. "I believe my King was about to fuck me."

"Hmm, was I now?" he asked, thrusting upward into my already leaking pussy.

"Yes," I breathed.

His hands cupped my breasts, and my head fell back. Like a pro, his fingers pinched, flicked and gripped my nipples hard enough to leave bruises, just the way I liked. My moan was loud and probably heard by anyone within a thousand feet of our home.

"So goddamn responsive to me, Maid," he growled in my ear. All I could manage was another moan as I rubbed my leaking folds shamelessly against his erection.

"Please," I begged.

He stood and unfastened his pants before sitting down, positioning me so his cock was at my entrance. His tip broke the surface, and my eyes rolled back as he glided his whole length into me until I was flush to his pelvis.

"Fuck, Red. So damn tight," he growled. I could hear his struggle not to cum right there. "You fit so perfectly around my cock."

"You fill me so good."

I rocked, and his hands gripped my hips firmly, steadying me as he moved his up, making himself go deeper. I began to move up and down his length as he buried his head in my chest.

His hot, wet tongue licked a trail to my breasts. As his tongue swirled around my nipple, I closed my eyes in ecstasy. When he bit down, I cried out and swirled my hips, eliciting his moans of bliss.

"Fuck, Red. You move around my cock so damn good."

I swirled and ground my hips deep as his tongue licked its way up to my mark. Electricity flowed through me as his tongue lapped over the sensitive area.

Oh Poseidon. I was about to blow.

His grip grew stronger as he thrust up roughly. His teeth grazed my mark and my body went rigid.

"Come for me, Maid." He thrust harder into me, holding me steady with his hands.

My body obeyed, and I convulsed and yelled out. I moaned when I felt his warm seed filling me while he grunted.

Slowly, we both came down from our orgasms. Neither of us moved. My head was now on his chest as he rubbed my bruised hips.

Chapter Thirty-Nine

TAKAR

The night was spent making love with my mate in every room and on every surface of the house. Now it was morning, and I had to go to my job.

Zaz, the girls, Finly, and of course, Bash, would be working on a few more houses today. Of all of us, only one had yet to find a mate, but we all knew he would soon.

As we approached the office, Simon stopped and looked at me. "I know no one can know we are working together, but I want to say I'm nervous."

I raised an eyebrow. "What about?"

"What if I lose my temper? Will I just randomly shift, you know… like in the movies?"

I laughed and shook my head. "Real life is not Hollywood."

He still looked concerned, so I patted his shoulder as he looked at me. "When we get angry, our lions do tend to want to come forward. It's instinct for them to take care of our problems. But you are always in control. Just like with your angry outbursts before, you do the same thing."

"Okay," he whispered, then turned toward his group of protesters. Raf and I continued to the building and made our way to our office.

"What the fuck is happening to my money?" a very angry boss yelled as we stepped off the elevator.

Oh boy.

I looked at the fire-red man before me and had to hold back a laugh at the literal steam coming from the man.

"I'm sorry, boss. I just got in. What seems to be the issue?"

"Have you not seen the stocks?" he growled.

"No. I haven't been to my desk."

"Well, they are dropping, and people are backing out of deals. Those damn protesters are ruining my business."

No dude, that's all you.

I resisted the smile wanting to form. My plan was working. Soon he would be asking us to do illegal things, and we would record it and feed it to the police. Simon had a twin who was a cop—correction,she was a detective—and she was geared up and ready to go.

As usual, we worked double time to get the day's tasks done early. It didn't take long for our boss to leave, too amped up to do the job. I smiled, knowing this was only the beginning. Raf cleared his throat.

"We need to go. You have a ceremony to attend."

My lips curved up into a smirk, and we headed out.

Simon was waiting for us when we got to the beach.

"I feel like I should be dressing up, but um, mermen, don't wear anything," I said through nervous laughter.

"Hey it saves the pocketbook," Raf said.

"True." I shifted, and the three of us swam to the castle.

The plan was to meet there. The men might not wear anything, but my Aria would be dressed to the nines.

Chapter Forty

ARIA

It didn't take long to get the two new houses going, even with clearing some trees to make more private plots. Zaz literally snapped the trees. No need for an ax. The houses were up with a little help from some magic, and the furniture would be here tomorrow.

"Okay MerQueen, we must get you ready. The MerKing has sent over your clothes," Cora said as she dragged me to the ocean. Mermaids didn't wear much, the men wearing nothing, but women obviously wore a bra.

A MerQueen wore special clothing designed by the MerKing over her bra. Takar would design more for me over time, but this one was from the current MerKing. He had one designed for his mate before she passed, and he decided I was worthy to wear it.

We moved to the cave, and I slipped the garment on.

It was stunning.

"The MerKing will love it," Cora said.

I looked down and into the mirror. The dress design was delicate and filled with sea life. A turtle, whale, seahorse, and crab were stitched into the purple and black fabric.

"Let's go," I said, and we headed to the castle.

The MerKing's guards were waiting when we arrived. I looked around as they escorted us and took in all the people filling the ballroom. Honestly, I didn't know if it was possible to fit more people in here. I smiled when I noticed Zaz and everyone already getting their instructions from the council.

"I must join them," Cora said, and I nodded.

"Your Majesty," the guard said as we entered the MerKing's chambers. The MerKing spun around to face me, a stunning smile playing on his lips.

"You look like a queen," he breathed. "My mate would have loved to see this on you, as would your parents."

A rogue tear fell from my eyes at the mention of my parents. He swam to me and wiped it away. "Don't cry, dear. You are strong and they are with you everywhere you go," he said. I nodded, unable to speak. "Now let's get this show on the road."

As I waited in my designated spot, arms wrapped around me. I immediately leaned back into the embrace. Takar nestled his face in the crook of my neck.

"You look fucking stunning," he purred.

I twisted in his hold until I was facing him. "Hmmm, can't wait for you to take it off me," I replied seductively. His tail automatically wrapped around mine. "Easy there, we have a ceremony to do."

"They can wait," he said as he nipped my mark.

I let out a moan and tightened our tails. His lips met mine, and I knew we needed to stop, but damn if I didn't want to.

Tilly came up and swatted him on the back of the head. His tail immediately released mine as he spun to see who had just hit him. Tilly laughed. Well, the whale equivalent.

I couldn't help but smirk myself.

"It's time," a merman said.

Takar took my hand, and we swam to our fate.

Chapter Forty-One

TAKAR

I was a nervous wreck, and now my head fucking hurt.

Okay, so I deserved Tilly's thwack on the back of the head, but still.

Now I was about to be crowned MerKing, and I knew very little about mermaids.

Obviously, the MerKing knew this and would likely have someone give me the full history and all that. If it wasn't for my Aria, I would be a mess.

Aria squeezed my hand. "You got this," she linked.

A trumpet went off, and the ballroom grew quiet.

"Thank you all for coming today. The world as we know it is changing and so must our leaders. As you know, my beloved mate passed before she could give me a child. After the accident that killed many, I gained a child in Aria. As I helped raise her, I taught her everything I would have taught my own child. She is gifted with the ability to speak with Poseidon, just as her father was, and her mate also holds the ability. Takar is a kind man, born human, turned into a lion while serving in his military. Now he is one of us. His friends have mated with many of our own. I am ready to step down and hand the throne to the next royal Mers. The Council and I have voted. Please let me introduce Aria and Takar, your new MerQueen and MerKing."

The crowd cheered, and the MerKing, well I guess the former MerKing, grabbed a beautiful crown. The design was flawless and incorporated the land, sea, and lion perfectly.

"With this crown, I hereby declare Aria your MerQueen."

Everyone cheered again. Then he was in front of me. My crown was identical to Aria's, but the design was taller and went all the way around. "With this crown, I hereby declare Takar your MerKing."

When the crowd cheered, I felt warm and fuzzy inside.

Not that long ago, I thought I was a monster and didn't want to do anything. I didn't feel I was worthy, but now I was a literal king.

The now-former MerKing removed his crown, and it was locked in a box. He stood before us and bowed, everyone else following.

"Your Majesties," he said.

My mind spun, and I had no clue what to do or say.

Aria squeezed my hand and spoke.

Chapter Forty-Two

ARIA

Holy shit, I was officially the MerQueen.

As everyone rose from their bows, I spoke for the first time as their MerQueen.

"My beautiful Mers. I am thankful and excited to be your leader. I will lead with the guidance of our god, Poseidon. Our direct guard has been chosen, and our home is a small island that belonged to my mother. Many of you know this as you helped us build. If we are not at sea, we can be found there. I am proud and honored to be your MerQueen, and my mate, though a bit dazed, is also honored."

Laughter filled the ballroom at the jab to their MerKing.

"Now let's eat, dance and have a good time," I said, then turned to my mate, who was smiling devilishly.

Oh snap.

Before I could protest, his lips were on mine as his tongue seemed to dig for gold in my throat. As much as I tried, I couldn't hold back a moan.

As if right on cue, Tilly was behind him, thwacking him yet again.

I laughed and so did everyone else. Takar growled and pulled me to him before nipping at my mark. I swatted at his shoulder, which only made him grip me harder. Struggling against him was pointless.

With a sigh, I relaxed into his chest as the slow music began to play.

Mer culture was interesting. Yes, the Mers just laughed at their leader, but it was in fun. A mate bond was supposed to be fun, and what just happened was just a dose of what humans called PDA.

THE REST of the afternoon was spent talking to Mers and having a good time. As usual, the food was on point. We went into the chambers while the Mers continued to party.

"Your Majesties. We need to know how you want your staff," one of the councilmen said.

"All staff shall keep their jobs as long as they remain loyal. We have our direct advisors and guards, but we are not putting anyone out."

"Of course." He made a note.

"I will teach Takar the ways of our kind," Titan said.

"Thank you," I said.

"I would have it no other way." Takar shook his hand.

"Tomorrow we will meet, and I can formally introduce my team at dinner." I announced.

"Of course, Your Majesty," Titan said.

I smiled at the title coming from him. It made me feel happy and proud. Never in my life did I think I would become MerQueen, but my mate has been through so much and he was now in a position of power with support he likely never thought possible.

With that, Takar and I left and headed home. We had unfinished business to attend, and my aching core was a testament to that.

Chapter Forty-Three

TAKAR

I was glad we were in mermaid form for the length of the ceremony and celebration, since I was sure to be sporting an erection.

The top Aria was wearing looked so amazing on her, almost like it was made for her.

How did I get so damn lucky?

As we entered the door to our house, I closed it, then pinned her against it. I nipped down her neck as she tilted her head, giving me more access. "Fuck, Red. I need you so damn bad."

"Then have me, my King."

Oh fuck. There was no way I was making it long enough to get us upstairs. I moved my hand down her body to the hem of her skirt, my hands seeking her panties so I could pull them down.

My breathing hitched when I found there was nothing underneath her skirt. Jesus.

"Hmm, love that there is no barrier," I growled. My fingers traced along her folds, resulting in a slutty whimper.

Oh fuck.

I pulled Aria into a kiss, and my hand moved around her sensitive spot. She reached and unfastened my belt before freeing my rock-hard cock. As soon as my pants and boxers hit the ground, I spun her around and spread her legs.

My hand made a clapping sound as I swatted her perfect ass before roughly rolling it. I pressed myself against her, then gripped her hair, yanking her head back. She moaned as my tongue moved down her neck from her ear to my mark. Her body shook instantly.

When her wetness coated my fingers, I nipped at her ear.

"So naughty. Tsk, tsk. My beautiful Maid." I bit at her neck, teasing my mark. "Your King never said you could cum."

"Mmm," she responded.

"I guess I will have to punish you nice and hard. Bring you to the cusp of orgasm, then leave you empty and on edge until I say you can cum again." I brushed my cock against her folds.

Chapter Forty-Four

ARIA

Oh fuck. This man was torture, and I loved every second of it.

I never knew I would love a man having this much control over me, but here we were. Though I trusted my mate with every part of me, so should I really be surprised that I was submissive to him?

Electricity coursed through me as his length brushed against me. My knees weakened with the anticipation of the hard fuck I was surely about to get.

My head was yanked back hard as his thick, long cock slammed into me.

"Takar," I yelled out.

He pulled back and slammed into me again and again. The force was so strong he was probably bruising me. But damn if I wasn't enjoying the sweet pain. I felt my orgasm coming, then suddenly I was empty.

His rough breathing against my neck sent chills down my spine.

"Nuh-uh. Not yet," he snarled.

I clenched my thighs and let out a moan. "Need you inside me."

He slammed into me again, making me cry out and shake. His hand moved and teased my clit as he thrust into me with wild abandon. I leaned back into him and my bud pulsed.

In seconds, his hand was gone, and I was empty again.

"Fuck. Need to cum," I whined.

"Oh, but you already did, Maid. Why should I let you cum again?"

Oh Poseidon, have mercy.

"I want to taste us mixed together," I moaned.

He plunged inside me and yanked my hair back as his tongue teased my mark.

I knew what he was about to do. I could feel it in every part of my being. His thrusts were rough and hard, just like I liked.

When his movements jerked and lost rhythm, I knew he was about to cum.

"Cum NOW," he ordered as his cock stiffened to concrete before pulsing his hot seed inside my core.

I wailed as my knees gave out from the intense release. The buildup gave my orgasm so much power I felt drunk.

Just as I was coming down, he bit my mark, making me come completely undone again. His movements never stopped.

As we both worked to catch our breaths, he slid out his sated cock before swirling his fingers inside my dripping pussy. He spun me around so I was facing him, and I wrapped my legs around his waist. As he placed his cum-covered fingers to my lips, I swirled my tongue around them like I would his cock. Then I took them into my mouth until I had every drop.

His cock returned to life and poked at my entrance, clearly wanting more.

His lips met mine, and his tongue explored my mouth, tasting us together. My eyes rolled back in the bliss. I swirled my hips and gasped as his length entered me again.

Takar brought out my inner slut, and I was a cum slut, to say the least.

Without warning, I bit down on his mark. He roared as his body shook with his sudden release.

"Fucking brat," he growled as he yanked my hair and returned the favor.

Oh fuck.

My yell fell mute on my lips as my orgasm hit hard and fast. A gush of cum soaked me and Takar. He looked down and ran his fingers through the wet substance.

Did I just squirt?

Chapter Forty-Five

TAKAR

Holy shit, I just made her squirt.

I licked up her release from my fingers, then lifted her so her legs were wrapped around my neck and my face was level with her sweet pussy. My tongue moved around her folds as I cleaned every last drop of the sexy squirt she just gave me. It was now my mission to get that to happen again.

Because fuck, that was sexy as hell.

I grazed her clit with my tongue, and she moaned so deep it went straight to my balls. My erection bobbed, ready to go.

Never letting up, I licked, sucked, and nipped at her bud as I carried her to our room. Her hands had a death grip on my hair and I relished it.

As my shins hit the bed, I bit down on her clit. I was immediately rewarded with her warm essence on my tongue. So damn delicious.

I tossed her onto the bed, then crawled over her, pressing my erection into her thigh.

"I will never get enough of you," I purred as I pressed my tip against her hole. Her wetness made my length glide in easily. Her channel tightened beautifully around my shaft.

Oh God. I closed my eyes in concentration, trying desperately not to cum.

"So damn tight, so damn perfect. Fuck Red," I moaned each word. She swirled her hips, and my balls drew up.

Fuck.

I pulled out of her, then slammed back in, making sure to go at the perfect angle to hit her sweet spot. She gripped my arms and wrapped her legs around me.

Breaking her hold on my arms, I leaned over her and cradled her head in my arms, using the position to push her down into each thrust.

My lips were on hers, swallowing her moans of ecstasy. The tingling in my balls increased, and I knew I was close. I broke my lips from hers and buried my face in her neck.

I smirked, then bit down on my mark. She screamed, and her channel strangled my cock as I pulsed my own release deep inside her warmth.

After every single drop was milked from my spent cock, I collapsed on the bed next to her. She immediately snuggled into my side and sleep consumed us.

Chapter Forty-Six

ARIA

I woke up comfortably in my mate's arms. Today, there was lots to do. I had to perform royal duties while Takar did more to take down the oil company.

My royal guards would be with me at all times when I wasn't with my mate. The same went with his guards, though the Simon situation complicated it for a bit, but all would work itself out.

Takar shifted slightly, and he laid a soft kiss on my head. "Morning," he mumbled.

"Hmm, morning." I snuggled in closer.

He chuckled and tugged me so I was lying on his chest before drawing me into a deep kiss. His phone rang, and he pulled away with a growl.

With our foreheads still touching, he answered his phone. His forehead creased as he let out a groan.

"I'm on my way," he said, then hung up.

"Sounds like something happened."

"Yeah, the boss is trying to pull some stunts. I have to get my evidence, then make a few calls. I'll meet you at the castle as soon as I can get away." He kissed me again.

"Okay, stay safe."

"Of course. I'm going to shower and text my guards."

I nodded and got up to cook us some breakfast.

Wanting to keep it simple since Takar had to leave, I pulled out some eggs, peppers, and sausage. I warmed the tortillas, and as soon as the food was cooked, I quickly rolled up eight burritos.

Arms wrapped around me as I was finishing, a tongue licking up my neck to my ear.

"Smells good, Maid," he purred.

"I made enough for you and the guys," I said, as I handed him the cooler with drinks and burritos. "You will have to buy lunch, well, unless I bring you some."

"Hmm. If my Maid brings me food, I may just have to give her a surprise." He nipped my ear.

"Then it's settled. I will bring you lunch." I stood on my toes to kiss him. "Now go take down the evil that is your boss."

As he turned, I swatted his ass and was pinned to the wall in seconds.

"Naughty, naughty, naughty. You, my Maid, will pay for that later," he growled, and I had to clench my thighs together.

Oh fuck.

He looked down and smirked before leaving.

I was screwed in the most blissful way.

Chapter Forty-Seven

TAKAR

When Aria smacked my ass, I almost lost it.

Fuck, I wanted to take her right then and there, but the call came from Raf. The owner of the oil company, my boss, was on a rampage at the office and was trying to do some shady deals. We needed documentation so we could end him once and for all.

The lunchbox was in a waterproof container so the swim to land wouldn't affect it. Raf was waiting for me at the beach and so was Zaz. Zaz obviously didn't work for the company, but we were using the protesters as a reason to pay him as "security."

Once on the mainland, I handed the guys their burritos and discreetly handed one to Simon, who was also already at the building. By the time we got to my office, the food was gone.

"Okay, your mate is a damn good cook," Raf said.

"I'll make sure to let her know," I said as I sat behind my desk. "Alright, so what is the boss doing?"

"Looks like he is trying to make some orders for low-grade

materials that are not graded for the use he wants. My internet scrub flagged it, and I called you."

"Okay, so we need to record him and get him to admit everything." I looked at my calendar. "Looks like we have a meeting in a bit, so hopefully we can get it. Simon's sister works in the police department, so she will be our point of contact."

"Sounds good."

I made sure my recorder was working, and we headed to the boardroom for the meeting. The recorder looked like a pen, so it was easy to get it past the man.

"Okay, so we need to cut some corners 'cause I am not making as much as I want. I don't care about doing things by the book anymore. I want my damn money."

Well, damn, this was about to be easy as hell.

"Boss, if we cut corners, eventually you will lose money with repairs and fines. Not to mention lawsuits," I said.

"I. DON'T. GIVE. A. SHIT."

"Okay. It's your ass, not mine," I said calmly.

"I want receipts by end of week."

"Yes, sir."

With that, he left.

I hit the button on my recorder and turned to look at Raf, who looked just as dumbfounded as I did.

"Make the call," I said. Raf got up and left the room.

Holy shit. I didn't think this would happen so soon, but here we were.

"Detective Grant will be here at eleven since the boss leaves in a few," Raf said.

"Nice, right around lunch."

Having a cop come here was a bit risky, but a detective wore plain clothes, and she knew to play a client if the boss showed up, which was doubtful.

I looked over the folder he left with exactly what he wanted circled. Fucking idiot.

"Did you see this?" I asked Raf, trying desperately not to laugh.

"No." He moved to the seat next to me. His eyes got huge, and he looked at me.

"Yeah, the man is dumb as hell."

"Understatement of the century."

A firm knock filled the room, and we both looked up to see a beautiful woman. She looked so much like Simon, which made sense, as they were twins.

"You must be Detective Grant." I stood and offered my hand.

"And you must be Takar and Raf," she replied as she took my hand.

"In the flesh." I released my grip.

"Please call me Petunia. What do you have for me?"

I pulled out my laptop and played the recording, then showed her the folder.

"Greed will get you every time," she sighed.

"Agreed."

"This is enough to get a warrant to plant devices here and in all his electronics. Once we have a good amount of evidence, we will arrest your boss."

"Thank you so much for helping us."

"Of course, my brother speaks highly of you. Though he seems to be holding some back. All I know is if he trusts you, then I will extend that trust to you."

The door swung open, making all of us jump. I relaxed when I saw it was Bash. My eyes narrowed when I saw his eyes. They almost seemed to glow and were locked on Petunia.

The hell?

I turned my head to the detective and noticed her eyes were locked on his. Their stare was intense, and I had to look away.

Aria and the rest of her guard came up to the door and looked between the pair.

"Mates," Aria linked.

Holy shit.

"Well, they need space to figure this one out, so let's bail." I pulled Raf out of the room, closing the pair in.

Bash was going to have to tell her everything and hope she would accept it and still help us. I knew it had been too easy. Now all we could do was eat lunch and hope for the best.

Chapter Forty-Eight

ARIA

Well, I'll be damned.

When Bash took off, I was pissed. He was supposed to be my guard.

Once we made it to Takar, I realized he had no control over his actions. His mate was here. A mermaid had a hard time functioning when they were around their unmarked mate.

I put the food in the break room and grabbed our portions before pulling Takar into his office.

"Looks like everyone will be mated soon. Assuming she accepts all of this," I said as I maneuvered Takar back into his chair.

As soon as his ass hit the seat, I was straddling him. His hand immediately moved to my waist.

With my arms wrapped around his neck, I leaned down and claimed his lips. His responding moan made my pussy leak in anticipation.

"Hmm, fuck, Red."

He firmly pressed my hips down so his erection pressed against me. I let out a gasp.

"I am going to pleasure you with my mouth," I whispered as I slid off his lap onto my knees, looking up to meet his beautiful eyes.

I undid his belt, button, and zipper, pulling down just enough to free his cock. My mouth watered at the sight.

So damn beautiful.

Starting with his balls, I sucked both in, making him grip his chair.

"Fuck," he moaned.

I released his balls and stroked his length before running my tongue up his vein. His hand gripped my hair as he thrust his hips.

"Hmm. Now, who is being naughty?"

"Open your sexy mouth and take my damn cock," he ordered.

Oh fuck.

He without a doubt just solidified who was in charge in the bedroom. I was leaking, my pussy craving him deep inside. But right now, he wanted my mouth.

Without a word, I opened my mouth and gagged as his tip hit the back of my throat.

"Fuck, Red. Fucking gag on my cock," he growled as he rammed his length into my mouth again.

I hummed my pleasure, and he moved in and out of me with a force that only meant his lion had a claw on the reins.

Tears ran down my cheeks as he gagged me over and over again.

I cupped his balls. He roared as his hot cum shot down my throat and his movements slowed. I sucked hard, making sure to get every last drop. Once I was sure I had it all, I released his tip with a pop.

He pulled me up so I was on his lap again.

"Fuck, Ariel," he huffed.

I smiled and claimed his lips. A hard knock stopped us before he was able to claim me again. My pussy ached for him. I buried my face in his neck.

"What the hell is this?" a male voice yelled.

I tensed and went to move, but Takar held me firmly in place.

"I am on my lunch, and enjoying some time with my fiance," Takar said calmly.

My heart soared. In lion and mermaid terms, we were married, but not yet in human terms.

"This is not a damn whorehouse."

In the blink of an eye, I was standing. Takar's pants were buttoned, and he was up and in the small man's face.

"Don't you EVER imply or call my fiance a whore. Do you understand me? I don't give a damn if you are my boss."

Takar was pissed, and not only that, but I now found myself face to face with my father's killer. He may not look like a killer, an asshole yes, but not a killer. My blood boiled in my veins as I plotted all the ways I could kill this man. Maybe death by siren or maybe pouring just enough poison in him to make his death long and painful. I was surprised to see the man looked scared as his body shook. His eyes dropped, and he took a step back.

"Don't let it happen again?"

"Let what happen again? My fiance bringing me lunch?"

"Fucking in my office."

"Last I checked, this room was my office."

"You know what I mean."

"No, I don't."

"Forget about it. I just came to grab my laptop." Without another word, the man practically ran out of the room.

My cheeks heated at almost being caught. Takar pulled me in and kissed me softly.

"Don't be embarrassed. I will never be ashamed of you, no matter what. Even if we get caught."

"Okay," I whispered.

"Now where were we?" he said as he looked at me with complete hunger in his eyes. But not hunger for the food that still sat untouched, hunger for me. I swallowed hard and flinched when I heard the lock to his door engage.

Fuck me.

Chapter Forty-Nine

ARIA

"Hmm. I know where we were. I was about to fuck that sexy little ass while I bent you over my desk." His tone was low and growly, the desire very evident. I swallowed hard as he stalked toward me.

He spun me around and folded me against his desk, his hand pressing my face down. As he lifted my skirt, his breath hitched.

"Fuck," he moaned. Swat. "So damn sexy." Swat. "Even sexier with my handprint on you."

He spread my legs with his knee. His body folded over mine as he cupped my breast with one hand while his finger pressed inside my ass.

I whimpered at the burn as he slowly began to stretch my hole. He pinched my nipple, and I relished the double assault.

"I'm going to take this ass nice and rough, make you scream in pain and bliss. Then once I fill this tight ass, I will eat my cum."

Oh fuck. I wiggled my butt, begging without words to be filled with his cock.

Two smacks filled the air as his hand made hard contact with my cheeks. Then he plunged his length into my quivering ass.

"Ah," I cried out.

"You like taking my cock, Maid?"

"Y-yes," I stammered as he slammed into me again and again.

His thrusts were animalist, and I sensed Slash was more in control than Takar. I let Red forward as we took his blissful beating.

Each slap made my cheek burn, but Poseidon help me if I didn't enjoy the hot sensation it left behind.

My ass was on fire.

Suddenly, my head was yanked back by my hair, and a hand wrapped around my throat. The pressure sent a jolt of electricity through me.

Oh fuck.

"Harder," I croaked.

He slammed into me with more force than I thought he could, his lion clearly giving him strength. Then his grip on my hair and neck tightened, and I saw stars as my orgasm slammed into me out of nowhere. My cry was muted by his hold on my neck.

"Hmm. Yes, squeeze my cock with that sexy ass," he growled, then bit down on my mark.

I came hard, my body tightening in every way imaginable as my cum flowed from me. His cock pulsed inside me as his warmth filled me. After he was empty, he dropped to his knees and licked my wet folds.

"Damn, so much cum, Maid. My little squirter," he hummed.

He licked and sucked until I was clean, then his tongue swirled my back entrance. The sensation made my legs shake.

His tongue dove in and licked like he was searching for treasure.

Oh fuck.

After several minutes, my body was ready to cum again.

"Slash," I moaned. "I-I'm about to—"

My release plowed to the surface. Takar was ready for it and took every last bit into his sexy mouth.

He stood and spun me around so I was facing him, then sat my bare ass on his desk. "So fucking delicious."

His lips met mine, and I swirled my tongue around his, wanting my own taste. I pulled away when my head began to spin with the need for oxygen.

"I have to get back," I breathed. He groaned. "Enjoy your lunch now that you've had dessert."

"I want to go with you," he whined.

"Soon. I promise. You have a takedown to do, and tonight you have dinner with the previous MerKing to talk about your duties. Then after that you have a mate to tie up and ravish," I said as I gripped his cock before turning and walking away.

Chapter Fifty

TAKAR

The thought of tying up my mate made my cock ache. It didn't help when she grabbed it either. I braced myself on my desk as all my blood rushed to my second head.

Damn.

The fact that I fought this still baffled me. She made me feel so damn good in every way.

It took me a few minutes to gather my wits. I quickly ate my pasta, then headed to the conference room. I let out a relieved sigh when I didn't find Bash and Petunia fucking. She was sitting on his lap while he checked over the evidence. He looked up at my entrance.

"Your boss really doesn't have a brain, does he?"

"Nope, pretty sure he is the Scarecrow from *The Wizard of Oz*, well, the evil version."

"Ha, yeah. He is something, that's for sure."

"So, uh, are you two good?"

"Oh yeah. Flou told me to take the day off, but I will be on the island tonight. My mate has to meet everyone and see her new home."

I smiled warmly. "How much have you told her?" I needed to know, so I didn't tell her something she didn't know and potentially cause an issue.

"That I am a mermaid and Aria is my MerQueen and your mate," he said.

"And that you are also a lion shifter who can talk to the god Poseidon," she finished.

Well, that about sums it up.

"Alright. I know you have lots of questions, and my mate and I will happily answer them tonight."

"Thank you," she said, smiling.

Honestly, it was a relief she was accepting this and even smiling about it like she wasn't fazed by it at all. "Bash, may I have a word?"

"Of course, Your Majesty," he said as he stood to follow. "I'll be back, my love."

He gave her a soft kiss, then followed me to my office. The smell of sex hit me, and I blushed.

Oops.

I reluctantly turned to look at Bash, who was smirking with a raised eyebrow.

"Well, I don't have to ask how your lunch was."

I narrowed my eyes at him, and he laughed.

"What did you need, Your Majesty?"

"Have you told her that she can shift?"

"Yes."

"What about the potential of becoming a lion?"

"What do you mean?"

"I mean, you are my mate's guard, the only one not to have the ability to shift into a lion, thus the only one who can't protect her on land. Yes, you can shift into a human, but you would get strength and agility from your lion."

"No, Your Majesty, I did not mention that."

"I suggest you do. It might be best coming from you. I will turn you, then you will reclaim her, which will pass the ability. But right now, I need you to help your mate with this case."

"Yes, Your Majesty."

"Good. You are dismissed."

With a quick bow of his head, he left.

Now to finish work so I could go to my mate.

Chapter Fifty-One

ARIA

How the hell did I get so damn lucky?

Almost getting caught was exhilarating. Of course, Bash now had his mate. Everything was working itself out.

"How was lunch?" Titan asked.

My cheeks heated, and I turned away.

"It was good. Looks like they are moving to the next step in taking the company down."

"That's good to hear. Takar is doing so much more than he realizes. Honestly, the oil industry isn't going anywhere, so we may as well have some control over it where we live. If he wants, we can financially back him in starting a business, taking over the oil industry here and doing it the right way."

"Oh wow. That sounds amazing. We can bring it up to him. Maybe use it to our advantage."

"How so?"

"The CEO can be anonymous. You be the vice president and the face. Start taking contracts and make his boss desperate. Maybe name it after my dad."

"I knew you would be an excellent MerQueen. Damn, I never even thought of that."

"That means a lot coming from you," I said as he pulled me into a hug.

"I know, sweetie, I know," he said, squeezing me tighter. "Now what all do I need to teach your mate?"

"Ha. Everything. We haven't exactly done a whole bunch of teaching, just um…"

"Fucking," he finished. I was going to combust into flames from embarrassment. "Don't be ashamed. Remember, I know how it goes, and I'm pretty sure lions have a high sex drive, too."

"I mean, you're not wrong."

He smirked. "Okay, so I need to teach him his duties and our history. Obviously, you can help with that too. You are the primary leader per the council and your family ties, but nonetheless he is MerKing and needs to act as such. Then there is your guard. Where is Bash?"

Oh yeah. I totally forgot to tell him.

"Well, he met his mate, so Flou gave him the day."

"No shit. Really?"

"Yes, she is human, but Simon's twin."

"Damn. Well, hopefully we'll meet her soon."

"I'll make sure of it."

We spent the rest of the afternoon going over everything, including the agreements and promises to other clans. Titan and I were going over the plans for the new MerSchool when I felt warm arms wrap around me.

Hmmm.

As I tilted my head, he quickly rewarded me with his hot breath over my neck, followed by a kiss.

"What are we looking at?" he whispered.

"The new school we have to approve."

"Looks beautiful."

"Shall we go sit? I would like to propose something to you, Your Majesty," Titan said as he gestured toward the office.

"Of course."

We made our way into the office and took our seats.

"Obviously, you have much to learn about our world and customs. I plan to rectify that soon, but I think you have something to offer us," Titan said.

"And what is that?" Takar took my hand in his.

I watched Takar's reaction as Titan told him about our idea. By the end of it, Takar was beaming. "I absolutely love the idea."

"Then tomorrow I will make it happen, boss," Titan said as he shook Takar's hand.

Fucking perfect.

Chapter Fifty-Two

TAKAR

Not going to lie, the thought of being the head of a business scared the shit out of me. But at the same time, I was practically doing it now, so why not make it official and do it the right way? And who better to know what's good for sea life than a mermaid?

Plus, I was going to have help.

Obviously, my employees would be my men and several mermen. I might consider hiring some humans, but I would be very cautious about who I choose, as I want to ensure the safety of my workplace. But that was a tomorrow issue. Tonight we had dinner.

We entered the dining hall, and my jaw dropped. Everything was beautiful. Pearls lined the walls and sat at the center of the grand table.

"Takar, do you know the significance of the pearls?" Titan asked.

"N-no."

"Other than being your mate's mom's name, they hold a

special value to our kind. Humans view oysters as food and some-thing to harvest for their jewels, but there is so much to them. An oyster bestows its pearl on the pure. If an oyster gives you its jewel, then you are respected by all."

Damn.

"But how are there so many?"

"Well, oysters are just like other sea life. Eventually they die and our hunters collect them, and the chaste harvest the pearl. Our clan has the highest numbers in the chaste. Your mate, her father, her mother, me, Cora, Bash, and Flou are only a few. It is said in a time of need, the chaste will free the masses."

Titan's words hit like a ton of bricks. As a human, I never knew the significance of an oyster. "What do you do with the dead oysters?"

"Only the pure are allowed to consume them."

"Understood." I took my place beside my mate at the head of the table. Servants moved about getting everyone drinks as they arrived. All our friends came. Bash led Petunia to us.

"Your Majesties, this is my mate, Petunia. I hope you will accept her into the clan," Bash said, his happiness evident in his tone.

I stood as my mate did, both of them bowing.

"Of course, please take a seat and enjoy the dinner," Aria said.

Soon, the food was placed before us, and Titan stood. Everyone fell silent.

"As you know, I am no longer MerKing, but I have full faith in my replacements. I want to present a toast to new beginnings and happiness among us."

Everyone cheered, and as we took our first bite, everyone else dug in. The food was amazing and unlike anything I had ever imagined. It still baffled me how they cooked underwater, but I figured I'd soon find out.

As the ocean grew dark, mermaids began to go home, and soon, it was only us and the guards.

"Well, I guess it's time to get to the island," Zaz said.

"You guys go ahead. Takar and I need to talk to Bash and Petunia," Aria said. They nodded and headed out. I could see the worry etched on Bash's and Petunia's faces. "Relax, it's nothing bad."

They visibly relaxed.

"Bash, have you discussed what I talked to you about earlier?" I asked.

"Yes, Your Majesty."

"Please call me Takar." I said. It was still so weird to be called Majesty.

"And how do you feel about it?" Aria said, directed at Petunia.

"Honestly, it's a lot, but just like I have a job to do, so does my other half. So if this is something he needs, then I will embrace it, too."

"A perk is strength and speed. A lion can be helpful in your line of work," Aria added, making Petunia smile.

"I never thought about that."

"Would you like to be turned tonight or tomorrow?" I asked.

"Can we do it tonight?" Bash said.

"If your mate is okay with it, yes," I said.

"Yes, that is fine."

We made our way to the island, and I turned Bash quickly so he could go be with his mate, and honestly, I wanted to ravish mine like I promised.

Chapter Fifty-Three

ARIA

My body shook with anticipation as we entered our room. I knew what was about to happen, and my pussy was already leaking.

Being tied up had been a fantasy of mine for a long time, and now I was about to experience it. Not only that, but doing it with my forever partner, my mate.

As soon as we were in the room, Takar's lips were on mine. He pressed against my body until I fell back onto the bed.

Hunger consumed his face, making me squirm under him.

"Hmm, if you are going to squirm like that already, I might just have to tie you up all the time," he growled.

Oh fuck.

A whimper escaped my lips as my legs fell open, silently begging for his cock. He looked down and smirked as he rubbed his fingers against my folds.

"So slutty for me. Hmm. So wet," he purred, then I felt the impact of his palm on my pussy.

Holy shit, I never knew that action could feel so damn good.

He reached over and grabbed a tie. After he secured my wrists together, he raised them above my head and tied them to the headboard. His hand moved down the knot to my throat, where he pressed down.

"Yes, harder," I begged.

His grip tightened, and he growled low in my ear.

"Does my Maid like being choked by her King?"

"Yes," I moaned.

He leaned over me, pressing his tip into my thigh as he whispered in my ear. "I am going to choke you until you see stars, then I will blow your mind with your orgasm as I breed that sexy hole."

Oh Poseidon, yes.

My eyes rolled back at the threat. I knew this was about to be hard and fast. The idea of being bred by this man was turning me on.

Who knew I would have a breeding kink?

I certainly had enough creampies, but the way he said it was like he was willing it to happen. Part of me thought it was too early, but I knew when the gods thought it was time, it would happen and only then.

His cock slammed into me, and I cried out at the pleasurable pain. He took a punishing pace, making me moan like a whore on Sunday.

My eyes rolled back as his grip on my neck began to cut off the air. I was on the verge of ecstasy as I tugged against my restraint.

"Nuh-uh, you are mine," he growled.

Without warning, he bit down on my mark and tightened his grip. My head spun from the lack of oxygen, my body shaking as I squirted my release all over him. The sensation of his cum filling me overwhelmed me.

As his hand released my neck, he pressed down on my clit and I cried out with another orgasm.

"Some say an orgasm during sex makes you more fertile," he purred, making me shudder.

Chapter Fifty-Four

TAKAR

I have no clue what came over me, but the way she responded told me she was very much into breeding.

All I could think about while I took her hard was her small frame with a baby bump. Her sexy body carrying our children. The image made my orgasm spiral forward and clearly hers as well.

After we both came down, I looked at my soaked body.

Damn, I wish I could lick that up.

"Maid, you made a mess," I teased.

"Hmm."

"Get on your knees and clean me," I ordered as I positioned myself so she could clean me while her wrists remained tied, but I freed her from the bedframe. Her tongue seemed to reach every divot of my body, making sure to get every last drop. The feeling of her tongue on my body was heaven.

I groaned as her mouth wrapped around my length, taking me all at once. "Fuck, Red."

She hummed, and my hands gripped her hair as I pulled her

into my pelvis, desperately wanting to be deeper. The way she licked, sucked, and nipped at my already sensitive cock was like she was auditioning for a porno.

Not that I minded. Her mouth was certainly porn worthy, just like the rest of her.

I reached down and stroked her lips, my eyes crossed at the sexy sight of her stretched to take all of me. "Fuck, I am about to cum."

She sucked harder, and my eyes rolled back as my cum jetted down her throat. My grip on her hair tightened, and I almost wondered if I was going to leave her with a bald spot.

After she was sure she had every last drop, she released my soft cock with a pop. As I collapsed onto the bed, I unbound her wrists and pulled her into my body.

"Damn," was all I could say before sleep took over.

Chapter Fifty-Five

TAKAR

I growled when I realized the bed was empty. A smirk spread across my lips when I thought about keeping her tied up next time. She would probably kill me, but I would make it up to her as I pounded and bred her into next week.

Why the fuck? All of a sudden, my mind was fixated on breeding her. Was it my time of the month or something?

I reluctantly got out of bed and put on some clothes. I had a meeting with Titan, then had to do my day job. Not to mention my training.

As I left the room, the smell of cinnamon and bacon hit my senses.

My Maid got up to make me breakfast. Her back was to me as she flipped the bacon in the pan. I walked up behind her and wrapped my arms around her. She immediately leaned into my embrace.

"Morning, mate," I said into her ear.

"Hmm, morning," she said, turning in my arms. I took her

lips in mine and moaned as her tongue dove in. The kiss was hard but filled with promises.

"Yesterday there were two, today there are three. Happy as can be, a baby will be."

I pulled back, breaking the kiss at Poseidon's words in my mind.

Judging by the look on Aria's face, she heard it too. My head spun as I desperately tried to figure out the meaning. My phone rang, and I picked up, my eyes never leaving Aria's.

"Yeah," I said.

"Am I on speaker?" Ursa asked. I pressed the button.

"You are now."

"I received a message from Poseidon."

"So did we," Aria said.

"What did he say?"

"Yesterday there were two, today there are three. Happy as can be, a baby will be," I answered.

"Holy shit. What did you two do last night?"

"The usual," I said matter-of-factly.

"So you fucked?"

"Yes," I said, getting slightly irritated.

"My message was, 'A family of three, a power within, protect the cherished so no one shall perish.'"

Fucking riddles.

"I'm really hating these riddles," I snarled. Aria reached her hand up and placed it on my chest, immediately calming me down.

"Aria is pregnant, and your child is the key to saving us from something," Ursa said.

Holy shit.

Chapter Fifty-Six

ARIA

My hand dropped to my belly, and tears filled my eyes. Tears of utter joy.

Takar wiped them away, then placed his hand over mine. "I'm going to be a father."

"Yes. Congratulations. This is huge news. It is yours to share, but Zaz knows. I will also say your guards need to know, but everyone else can wait until you are ready," Ursa said.

"Okay," I said, and the line went dead.

Holy shit. Was I in heat last night or something?

My head was spinning, but honestly, I couldn't be happier. I was going to be a mom, and my mate was going to raise them right along with me.

"I'm staying home," Takar said.

I swatted him on the shoulder. "Oh, no you're not. I may be pregnant, but I am perfectly capable of functioning. Besides, I will have my guards, plus a few extra. I now have to find a nanny and do all that, plus plan an announcement to remember. You go do your job. I will do mine. If you need me to, I will check in. But I will not be coddled. Understood?"

"Understood," he replied.

"Good, now eat your breakfast and get."

"As you wish, my Maid."

A smile played on his lips that had my pussy leaking. I just bossed him around, and I was going to pay for it dearly later.

As soon as he was out the door, I called Cora.

"Hey, you need us?"

"Yes, get my guard. Have Takar's meet him at their spot. Call for Titan as well."

"As you wish."

One thing I made sure of is that my friends and guards referred to me with respect, but they were not required to call me MerQueen or Your Majesty unless in public.

Well, public with mermaids, not humans.

Within minutes, everyone was at my place.

"Okay, so you sounded like you had news. And Miss Ursa looks like she knows something. Spill it," Cora said. I couldn't help but laugh at her demanding tone.

"We received a message from Poseidon. And, well, last night when we mated, I was literally mated," I said, not wanting to say it out loud.

"Wait, you're…?" Cora started.

"Yes. As of this morning, according to the god Poseidon, I am with child." I placed my hand on my belly.

"Not just any child, the Cherished," Ursa added. I heard a gasp and looked to see Titan with his eyes wide and his hand over his mouth.

"What is it?" I asked.

"Prophecy of war. Sirens and mermaids. A MerQueen granted powers through her unborn child, a child touched by the gods, a child destined to rule all Merkind."

Holy shit.

"Well, damn," Cora said. "Looks like I will be planning a celebration!"

I laughed and shook my head.

"Yes, you do, and now I have to find a nanny."

"If I may, my mate and I had a nanny picked out, despite us not expecting. She is older now and has a daughter who helps. So why not hire the pair of them?" Titan said.

"If you trust them, then I see no reason I shouldn't," I said.

"Cora, do you remember Sandy and her daughter Bay?"

"Yes," she replied.

"Bring Aria to see her and get acquainted."

Chapter Fifty-Seven

ARIA

"Okay, so the new plan is to arrange a celebration announcement and to meet the nanny. The rest can wait," Cora exclaimed. I couldn't help but smile.

Mermaids aren't pregnant for long, well, not nine months like humans.

We preferred to have babies in human form. Both were just as painful, but it was easier as a human. Not to mention, we never knew what form the baby would come out as.

If the baby came out as a mermaid then you needed to be near water. Seeing human doctors for pregnancy was a no go unless approved by our monarch. Titan had one doctor he let us use, two if you count the trauma specialist. Needless to say, I would have to get established soon since I would only be pregnant for a few months.

We arrived at the castle and were greeted by Merfolks, who bowed at my entrance. The staff was buzzing with activity as they redid the castle to account for two monarchs instead of one. This all still seemed so surreal.

A butler came to me and bowed. "Your Majesty. Do you need anything?"

"Yes, can you send for Sandy and Bay?"

"Of course." With a quick bow, he left.

The throne room was buzzing with activity, and I was tired. Mermaids got symptoms pretty quick too, yet another reason to announce soon since it wouldn't be a secret for long. My staff were sworn to secrecy on many things, but this would be hard to contain.

"Cora, can we have this room clear for our guests?" I asked.

"Of course. I will make it happen," she replied, then went over to the supervisor. Within seconds, the room was clear except for me and my guards. I sighed with relief.

"Are you starting to have symptoms?"

"Yeah, I may be in human form more often to help," I mumbled.

"Of course. Once it is announced, it will be easier to arrange land meetings. We can use the new business office."

Well, damn. This is why she is my right-hand man. Or woman in this case.

"That sounds like a great idea."

A thought hit me. What if there was a way for us to communicate like I can with Takar?

"Ursa?"

"Yes, Aria."

"Is there a way to give us a way to mindlink at all times? Not all mermaids, just my guard, Takar and his guard, plus Titan."

"There is a way, yes. I can do the spell, but only Poseidon can grant the spell to work. As a human witch, well, you know what I mean, my power to you is limited."

"How do you mean?" I asked.

"I mean, if I was a mermaid, a true one, it would work better and drain me less."

"But you aren't a mermaid, not without a spell."

"Exactly."

"The trident's power is sacred. My blessing is given. Change the witch, and links shall be given," Poseidon's voice said. I gasped, then the voice continued. "Sunset is the key to unlocking the powers of the prongs, and by morning, it will be done."

Everyone was looking at me. "Poseidon has spoken. By sunset, I need the trident."

"I will send for it. Titan will have to retrieve it, as he has not given its location to us yet," Cora said. I nodded.

The door opened and a young lady, who I assumed was Bay, and an older lady, entered the room. They bowed before the older woman, Sandy, spoke.

"Your Majesty. You called us to see you."

"Yes, I did. Titan has spoken fondly of you. What I am about to tell you is not to leave this room until it is announced."

"Yes, your Majesty," they said in unison.

"Takar and I are expecting a child. Not just any child, but one touched by the gods and the key to saving us." The pair gasped. "I want the pair of you to be our nannies."

The smiles that spread across their faces were priceless. "I would be honored, Your Majesty," Sandy said.

"As will I, Your Majesty," Bay added.

"Good, then the job is yours, effective immediately. We need the party planned, and you will have to spend time on land at my home or your MerKing's office. Be at my island tonight."

They bowed and headed off to start their job. They needed to be linked, since they would be caring for our child. Now I needed to do my own duties so I could finish in time for sunset.

Chapter Fifty-Eight

TAKAR

The morning was interesting, to say the least. Petunia was on the case and set up all the bugs needed to take down my boss. Everything was ready, so now we just had to wait.

I did my normal tasks, then headed to my new office to get everything organized and ready to go. I also had to get my training from Titan.

"Be at our island at sunset, Poseidon spoke to me," Aria linked, and I smiled. Her lion Red played back memories to Slash, and I smiled even more.

My mate was so fucking genius.

I walked through the doors to my new office and was greeted by a few Merfolk.

"Titan is waiting in your office, Your Majesty," one of the mermen said.

"As long as we are in the human world and you are acting as my employee, please call me boss."

"Of course, Your—"

I raised an eyebrow.

"I mean, boss."

I nodded my approval and entered my office. My jaw dropped as I looked at the setup. It was like the man pulled my wishes from my mind.

Damn.

I took my seat as I looked around the room, taking in every detail. "You did very well, Titan."

"Thank you. I like to fancy myself good at guessing people's likes."

"Well, you hit the nail on the head here."

"As much as I love the praise, Takar, shall we get to it?"

"Of course."

The afternoon was spent going through documents and making proposals to companies for contracts. Then, of course, my history lessons.

Mermaids had a fascinating past, and I wanted to know it all. Every sea or ocean had up to five clans, the smaller ones only having one, some having three. Only one had five. We had three.

The customs were similar to those of Native Americans, which is my upbringing. Then he spoke of the sirens and how they came to be. A mermaid betrayed her MerKing, her mate, and was cursed by a witch. She was pregnant, and the curse passed to her child, and as her kids had kids, it continued to pass to everyone.

The part I found fascinating was that the curse could be broken. A siren could choose the path of right, but they were isolated and hidden from good, so not many did. Sandy was one Titan's mate had been able to save before her death.

Zaz, Raf, and Simon took everything in as well since they were not born mermaids, so they, like me, were unfamiliar with the history.

And to think this was only the tip of the iceberg.

One thing I looked forward to was meeting other clans, and

as MerKing, that was going to happen soon. Many would visit to meet the new royal family and celebrate our child.

"Shall we head to the island?" Titan asked.

"Yes," I replied.

Chapter Fifty-Nine

TAKAR

As I came to the shore, I noticed my beloved mate still in the water, holding a trident in her grasp.

What the?

Everyone gathered directly in front of Aria, including Ursa and Zaz.

"Aria, what is going on?" I asked as I swam next to her.

"Poseidon is granting Ursa and Zaz the permanent gift of being mermaids. And soon all those close to us will be linked like us." Her eyes sparkled as she spoke. I looked around and saw all our guards, Titan, and two mermaids I hadn't met and I assumed were the nannies.

Well, damn.

The sun began to set, and Aria placed the trident flat on the surface of the calm sea with the tips pointing at Ursa and Zaz. Light moved across the surface, never breaking as waves formed.

My eyes widened as I watched Ursela and Zaz rise out of the water, their backs arching as light surrounded them and their legs sealed together as their tails took hold. The light then lowered them into the water.

Shock coursed through me at the beautiful transformation. I watched intently as the light traveled and enveloped everyone. This time, no one was lifted from the water, but light surrounded everyone's faces. Orbs formed and traveled toward Aria and me, each orb splitting in two before reaching us.

"Open," Poseidon said.

I complied, and the orbs entered my body. A jolt of power surged through me, followed by voices, the voices of the people around us. A gasp escaped my lips, and I looked at Aria, who was smiling. The trident was now upright.

"You are connected and strong with your trusted few. You can speak to one, two, even all at your will. If you stay open, they can call on you, a silent knock on your consciousness, and you can answer."

I looked at my mate, confused about the meaning. "Basically, we can talk to whomever we please, but our thoughts are private unless we will them to the others. This means when they want to reach us, if our barriers are up, we will sense their desire to speak to us and we can answer."

Why couldn't Poseidon just say that?

"Everyone, please rest. We will enjoy the newfound ability tomorrow. Go be with your mates," Aria said.

In seconds, we were alone, and my mate was snuggled into my chest. "Take me home so you can fuck me, then let me fall asleep in your arms."

With pleasure.

I growled and scooped her up and carried her to our house.

The new power in us must be affecting her as much as it was affecting me. My cock was leaking, and her scent was flaring with the spices of her arousal.

Fuck, she smelled delicious. If she wasn't already pregnant, she would be by the time I was done with her.

Chapter Sixty

ARIA

When the power pulsed through me, I thought for sure I was going to cum. I sensed it affect Takar, but knew it hit me harder. Probably because I was pregnant. All I knew was I needed to be claimed again.

Once in our home, I was stripped of my clothes and placed on the bed. I watched hungrily as Takar quickly took off his clothes. His hard erection slapped his belly.

My mouth watered, and I squirmed. He smirked knowingly and stalked toward me like he was the hunter and I was the hunted.

The look in his eyes told me I was going to be dominated in the most carnal way. My pussy leaked at the idea.

He sniffed the air and growled low and deep. "Your arousal is making me feel drunk, and I haven't even had a taste yet." His tone was so thick with desire, my body shook.

Fuck me.

His palm cupped my leaking pussy. I let out a moan as his fingers brushed my slit. Takar's lips were on mine, swallowing my erotic moan. Every part of me he touched was on fire in the best way.

"I need you inside me," I begged.

"Tsk, tsk, patience Maid. You will have me bottoming you out soon enough, but your King needs to taste you first," he said seductively.

Oh fuck.

I leaked more, and I wondered if I would have anything left for later.

A gasp escaped me as two of his thick fingers slid into me. He slid down my body until his face was at my clit. His tongue swirled my nub, and I gripped the sheets like my life depended on it.

I was already flying, and he had only just started.

The way he moved slowly with everything he did was driving me wild. I was in sensory overload, and when I came, it was going to be messy.

Though I knew Takar would relish it.

My back arched with every swipe of his tongue and the glide of his fingers. Fuck, I needed him so damn bad.

I whimpered, needing his cock inside me. His mouth moved to mine as his fingers continued to glide in and out. His tip brushed against my clit, and I cried out.

"Need you now," I begged.

He chuckled devilishly, then slid his length in slowly until his hips were flush to me.

"Fuck," he moaned. "So damn tight."

His pace was painfully slow. So slow I was able to feel every vein as it pulsed inside me.

Now I like a rough fucking with some pain, but this wasn't just fucking, this was making love. I was carrying his child, and we were so much more powerful than before.

His fingers danced around my clit. I pulled him to me, needing to be close to him. He let out a moan as my nails dug into his back. His speed increased ever so slightly, and my body was ready to cum.

"Hmm, yes," I breathed, and I squirmed beneath him.

"Fly," he ordered as he thrust hard into me, his warm seed heating me from the inside.

I cried out as I came so hard I almost threw him off of me. My release seemed never to end, and every muscle in me ached. He slid out of me as I came down ,and in seconds, I was asleep in his arms.

Chapter Sixty-One

TAKAR

The slow lovemaking drove me wild, but fuck if it wasn't exquisite. Sleep came fast, and before I knew it, it was time to get ready for the day.

I kissed the top of Aria's head, and she snuggled in deeper. I chuckled. "My sweet mate, we have to get up."

"No," she said, nestling in.

I swatted her ass.

"Nu-uh. Don't be a bad girl. I would have to punish you later."

The responding moan and flare to her scent told me she liked that idea very much. Not going to lie, I too liked the idea.

"Takar," Titan's voice said in my head.

"Yes," I replied, managing not to jump at the sudden sound.

"We need to visit our office to check on contracts before you go into work."

"Getting ready now," I replied, then shut off the link.

"Aria, as much as I want to cuddle you and ravish your body until you can't see straight, I have business to attend to. But tonight," I said as I repositioned myself over top of her perfect body. "Tonight I will fuck you until you see stars." She whimpered and squirmed beneath me. "Now go get ready to plan our announcement with our nannies."

She groaned, but rolled over and got out of bed. We took turns washing each other in the shower, then headed to shore.

Our various guards were waiting. I pulled her to me and claimed her mouth with mine.

"I love you," I whispered.

"I love you," she breathed.

I entered the water and shifted, my guards following. It was amazing to watch Zaz shift without a spell. We dove into the water and headed to the mainland.

"How does it feel to shift naturally?" I asked.

"Fucking amazing. Those spells make you tired as fuck, man. But now it's not an issue. Plus, the sex is on point."

"Had you guys not let your mermaids take control before?"

He shook his head. "When you shift under a spell, that kind of stuff doesn't work."

"Huh, interesting."

"That's what I said. But it's all in the past now."

"Indeed."

Once to shore, we all shifted and headed to my business. Titan was already waiting.

"Ah, boss, you made it. Here are the replies from after you left the office yesterday and early this morning. It looks like at least a dozen companies are ready to break contracts and come to us. With your permission, I would like to send over our contract and see what they say."

I looked at the list and smiled. These were the big companies that were my boss's main income, and soon they were going to be mine. I smirked.

"If they agree to our terms or within reason, then they will be signed by the end of day."

"Of course, boss," Titan said.

"If they counter, let me know immediately."

"As you wish."

I got up and Raf, Zaz, and I headed to the office. When I sat at my desk, I got a text. It was my boss.

> Coming in a little late. Our meeting will be at 11.

I sent a thumbs up and got to work as if nothing was happening.

It didn't take long for the boss's desk phone to start ringing and his email to keep dinging.

"Judging by the calls and emails, I'm guessing things are happening," I linked to Titan.

"Yes, ten of the twelve so far. They love our contract and our mission so much they aren't countering at all."

"Good."

I looked up when I heard the front door open, and my boss headed to his office. He always checked on everything before our meetings, and this was about to get interesting.

Zaz moved closer to me, and so did Raf. Both men were standing on either side of me, ready to attack in my defense.

"Petunia, be ready," I linked.

"Recording now."

"WHAT THE FUCK!" my boss exclaimed, making me tense.

Yep, he was mad.

"WHO THE FUCK IS PEARLY COVE?" he yelled as he slammed open my door. I looked up at him with a confused expression on my face.

"Who?" I asked.

"That's what I want to know. I lost twelve damn contracts in one day. How the fuck does that even happen?"

"I'm not sure, boss. Forward me the messages and I will look into it," I lied.

"No, *you* are going to fix it, or you are fired. I want every remaining contract finished by any means necessary so I don't lose any more money. Fuck regulation, just get it done."

And there it was.

"I'll need you to sign the forms for the parts," I said as I placed the prepared forms. He was so mad he wasn't even suspicious of the fact I had them ready.

These were the contracts that didn't care about legal stuff, so these were the bait. He would be arrested, and they would be investigated and shut down.

Win-win.

He slammed the pen down after he signed everything, then charged out of the office. Just like that, this company was no more. Petunia would arrest him as soon as the warrant was signed.

My tension disappeared. Aria needed to see this.

I smiled warmly at Petunia as she came into the office.

"Petunia, can you arrest him at the office tomorrow when my mate is here to see it?"

"Yes, Your Majes…I mean Takar."

"Thank you."

She grabbed the folder and left without another word. I shut down my computer and headed to my new office to start our plans and my lessons.

Chapter Sixty-Two

ARIA

"I like the idea of having the ceremony at the castle, but the party on land. The problem is, where on land would everyone feel safe?" I said.

"We don't want everyone coming to your island. It is sacred to you, and the human world is a mess. Many Merfolk won't go to land. Some live too far and would be out of sorts. Not to mention, the more who shift, the more likely one is to get caught," Cora said.

I leaned back and sighed. Damn, she had a point.

"Okay, but we're having an after-party," I grumbled.

"Now that we can do," Bash said.

Everything for the party was picked out, and a date was chosen. All anyone would know is a celebration was happening. Which could be anything, our union, a new recipient of a pearl or, of course, us expecting a child.

"Alright, it is settled. We celebrate tomorrow and will send announcements tonight to the other clans," Takar announced.

"I'm exhausted. If you all will excuse me, I would like to go home and rest." I fought back a yawn.

I swam home, my guards on my tail. My lion was itching to be let out, so I decided I would sleep in lion form as I basked in the sun.

As MerQueen, I knew I could not be left unprotected without my mate, so I lay against a tree while my guard rested in their lion forms nearby.

Soon I found myself belly up, enjoying the sun's punishing rays. I frowned when the light dimmed and I felt someone over me.

Slowly, I cracked my eyes open and smiled when I saw Slash towering over my vulnerable body.

"Look at you, ready to be dominated by your King," he growled in my mind.

"I'm always ready for you," I purred. I could feel his smirk.

"Indeed." He rubbed his face against mine. "Hmm. I promised to fuck you, and I plan to collect. And I have a surprise for you tomorrow at eleven, so you will be coming to work with me."

Oh fuck. That sounded divine. Not only was he going to fuck me until I saw stars, but he had a surprise for me. I had no clue what it was, but something told me it was big.

"Good, cause we have our first appointment at seven."

He pulled back and looked at me. "Well, I guess we need to get home and get to bed since we have an early day," he said as he started walking away. "No time for play."

I jumped and nipped at his flank. "No, you promised. And I have been waiting all day."

He laughed and took off toward our place with me hot on his tail.

Chapter Sixty-Three

TAKAR

Teasing Aria would never get old.

Obviously, I was going to fuck her—seeing her belly up had my head spinning with lust. Before I knew it, I was in my lion form, taking all of her in.

As soon as the house came into view, I shifted and was in our room in seconds, my clothes already on the floor.

Aria pounced on me and nipped at my ears and neck. My cock responded immediately.

In seconds, I flipped us so she was pressed against the mattress. Without foreplay or warning, I slammed my full length inside her, making her curse and yell out my name.

"Hmm, love it when you whisper sweet nothings," I growled. I pulled back several inches before slamming back into her, making sure to hit her sweet spot. Her hands gripped my arms as I plunged deep into her over and over again.

As much as I wanted to draw this out, we both needed rest. Her legs tightened around me, and I knew she was getting close.

"Yes, take my cock like a good Maid. Then take my essence like a good girl."

That did it.

My cock was gripped in a vise-like hold as she yelled out, her body twitching with every wave of her orgasm. The sensation and sight sent my own orgasm rushing to the surface. I roared as I slammed into her harder than before as stream after stream of my cum filled her hot channel.

After her walls released their hold and my cock stopped twitching, I lay next to her and pulled her into me.

"Sleep," I whispered, and she snuggled into me. Soon, her soft snores filled the room.

I woke up, and Aria wasn't in bed with me. I shot up and looked around.

Where the fuck was she? I couldn't feel her in the home, so she had left already.

My anger boiled. I looked at the clock, and we still had plenty of time before we needed to go. I charged outside, not caring that I was naked.

A sigh of relief gusted out of me when I saw her sitting with Cora near the trees.

Thank the gods.

My strides toward her were long and projected my displeasure and fear. Cora's eyes bugged. She hastily got up and headed to the shore to wait.

Good thinking.

"Slash, wha——"

My lips claimed hers. She melted into me and let out a contented moan.

"You were not in bed when I woke," I growled.

"I-I'm sorry. It won't happen again."

"Good."

My naked body left no secrets, and my erection was leaking. My eyes closed as her hand wrapped around my length and pulled up.

Fuck.

"Let me make it up to you," she whispered.

I opened my eyes to see her on her knees with my tip against her lips. I moaned like a virgin on prom night as she swallowed me whole. Oh gods.

My hand gripped her hair, and my hips thrust, wanting more. When she twisted and pulled at my balls, I stumbled back into the tree.

This was going to be over fast.

Her teeth grazed the sensitive vein on the underside of my shaft.

"Red," I growled as my cum shot down her hot throat.

Spurt after spurt, she swallowed and sucked. My grip softened, and I ran my hand down her face in a caress.

How did I get so damn lucky?

Chapter Sixty-Four

ARIA

I knew when I felt Takar's worry and frustration that he needed a release or he would be a grouch all day. Don't get me wrong, I wanted to be punished, but we had things to do and I knew it would come later.

It wasn't like I did it on purpose. Cora had a question and wanted to hang out, just the two of us, and I missed it just as much. The thought of leaving a note or waking Takar to tell him never crossed my mind.

Now we were on the mainland, heading to our appointment. The approved OB always saw us before or after normal hours, so there was no one around. He smiled as we entered the office.

"I hear congratulations are in order," he said.

"Apparently so."

"I have the ultrasound machine set up, so let's take a look."

I lifted my shirt and lowered my shorts enough for the doctor to perform the test. A smile spread across my lips as the small image of our baby appeared.

"Looks like the little one is measuring like they should for your kind. A healthy pregnancy, and it appears to be human right now."

It wasn't uncommon for a baby to shift while in the womb, so being human now didn't mean much.

I looked at Takar, who had tears in his eyes. His happiness was radiating off him.

The doctor printed off a few photos, and we headed out.

"How are you feeling?" I asked.

He looked down at me and placed his hand on my belly.

"More happy than I ever thought I could be. I got you, my mate, and soon I will have a child."

We were in the bathroom, so I did a partial shift to place the meds and photos in my tail pouch. Not all mermaids had it, but if you were lucky enough to have one, it came in handy when shifting. Once I was human again, we headed to the office for my surprise.

Takar sat at his desk with me on his knee. Zaz and Raf stood by our side, while the rest of the guard waited outside so as not to draw attention.

A fat man came in, looking pretty pissed off, and his heated glare met Takar's.

My lion grew restless, not liking the way he was looking at our mate.

"Easy," Takar linked as he rubbed small circles on my back.

"Did you find out who took my contracts?" the fat man barked. Takar smirked.

"Yes. I took them," he said calmly.

"No, you work for me," he growled.

A warning growl escaped my lips before I could hold it back.

"Not anymore. Pearly Cove is mine and my fiance's business. All we did was propose legal options and poof, they jumped ship from your crooked ways."

"You will pay for this," he growled as he moved closer.

I stood, and my eyes shifted to my lion's and back, Zaz and Raf right next to me while Takar watched the scene unfold.

Not going to lie, he looked rather pleased with me, and my lion liked it very much.

"If you knew who I was, you would be cowering before me. You are a rat, and where I come from, you would be rotting in the ocean for your crimes," I sneered.

The door slammed open, and I sensed Petunia immediately.

"Sir, you are under arrest," she said as she slapped her cuffs on his wrists. I stopped her before they could leave.

"You should be happy you are in the prisons provided here and not the ones I provide," I threatened.

Once they left, I turned to Takar. His face was a sight to see, and pride, happiness, and arousal shone in his beautiful eyes.

"Do you like your surprise?" he asked, his tone deep and sensual.

"Yes," I whispered as I climbed onto his lap. "And I know my father would be—no, is—proud." I claimed his lips, faintly aware of the empty room.

My mate gave me closure. Gave me revenge. Now I was going to ride him until the next renter of this space would only ever be able to smell our sex.

Chapter Sixty-Five

TAKAR

Watching my mate handle my ex-boss was hot as hell.

As soon as her gaze hit mine, I knew what was about to happen and ordered everyone out. My mate needed to fuck me until the sun went down.

In a haste, our clothes were off, and she rubbed her folds deliciously over my throbbing cock. I gripped her hips as I guided her so my length slid deep inside her. She tilted her head back and let out a slutty moan.

I grunted as I thrust up into her. "Fuck Red," I moaned.

She rocked her hips, then circled them, sending my cock into overdrive.

"Hmm. I have to thank my mate somehow. He gave me the best gift."

"Revenge is sweet, but nothing compares to you, Maid."

"Fuck," she breathed.

My thrusts were relentless as my arms wrapped up her body until my hands rested on her shoulders so I could push myself deeper. I nestled my face into her neck, taking in her scent as I licked and sucked at my mark.

She nuzzled her face into my neck as she gave her mark the same erotic treatment. I could feel my orgasm trying to break free. With a loud, deep growl, I bit down on my mark as I freed my release.

As soon as my cock stopped spurting my seed deep inside my mate, I stood up and bent her over the desk before diving back in.

"King," she cried out. "Hmmm, fuck yes. Harder."

I gave it to her. I smacked her ass before yanking her head back by the hair as I nipped my mark again. My free hand moved up her torso, stopping at her perfect breasts. I flicked and pinched her erect nipples.

"Yes," she breathed.

My hand continued until it found her throat.

"Choke me."

I growled my pleasure at her command as I applied sweet pressure.

"Make me see stars," she groaned.

Oh gods. My thrusts grew quicker, harder, as my grasp around her neck tightened. I was about to blow again.

"Cum, now," I ordered as I tightened even more.

Her body jerked as her walls tightened around my pulsing cock. I released my grip as I struggled to stay standing.

Just as I was about to pull out, she bit down on my mark.

"Fuck," I cried out, then bit down on hers, making her squirt all over me. My lion purred at the sight, and yet another orgasm exploded from me.

I collapsed onto my chair, my body buzzing and exhausted from the back-to-back releases. Leaning back in my chair, I looked at my beautiful, well-fucked mate.

"Come sit on my face so I can clean you."

<h1 style="text-align:center">Chapter Sixty-Six</h1>

ARIA

His order to sit on his face almost made me cum all over again, but I quickly complied. He sucked and licked me until I was clean, then spun me so I could clean myself off of him. I gasped when I felt his tongue press into my ass.

Poseidon have mercy.

"If I wasn't so well fucked right now, I would take this sexy hole right now."

Fuck. Part of me wanted him to, but the other part of me was exhausted, and we still had to get home.

"Tonight," I whispered. "Or maybe I will take what is mine now."

His cock twitched. I knew he would not be able to resist.

"Damn you," he growled as he slowly slid his length into my tight ass.

I would never get enough of this man, in any form.

NEARBY CLANS ARRIVED to celebrate with us. They didn't know what yet, but no one refused a party when invited. The royalty greeted us with respect, and of course, a few questions. Which was to be expected with a lion shifter mating with a mermaid.

My guard was on a rotation so they, too, could enjoy the food and company. Merkids would take trips with their school and visit the nearby clans, so a lot of us reconnected with long-lost friends. Everyone was so accepting of Takar, and it made my heart warm with happiness.

The crowd gathered around, and I stood at the head of the table, Takar standing with me.

"As you know, we called you here to celebrate. What you don't know is what we are celebrating. The gods themselves have touched this treasure, and we are happy to announce that MerKing Takar and I are expecting our first child."

The room exploded with cheers, clapping, and high-fives. This baby wasn't even born yet and was already so loved.

A loud alarm blared through the waters, and our guard was instantly in a circle around us.

A merman swam quickly over to Titan, who stood at the front, just like the warrior he was born to be. "Lord Titan, sirens have entered the grounds."

"Go to the emergency shelter," I ordered, and everyone left for the safe room as we stayed to deal with the threat.

"You should go too," Takar said.

I looked at him and frowned.

"No," I said matter-of-factly.

"But——"

"No buts. I am no coward. I am pregnant, yes, but remember our child holds powers and we can't use them if I am not here."

Takar sighed and nodded. He knew I was right. As we waited, I found it interesting that none of the sirens were trying to call. That was new.

A pair of sirens appeared in the distance, and they swam at a normal pace, not one poised for attack.

Once in front of us, they tilted and bowed their heads. "Your Majesties. We come in peace seeking asylum."

Well, I'll be damned.

I pushed past my guard, Takar moving with me.

"Why should we spare you?" I asked.

"You know the story of the siren. We did not choose this life. It took us years to escape the clutches of our leader. We are outcasts, refusing to do their dirty work, but we know their plan and have come to get your blessing and warn you," one of them said.

Sirens were ugly creatures, so as not to be tempting to good mermaids. Their skin was gray and filled with wrinkles. Their scales were dull and looked like dead attachments. And their hair was like straw. But if given our blessing, they would take their true mermaid form. Just like Sandy had.

"They are truthful. They are valuable. Invisible and discarded, they won't be missed. Plans revealed help in the fight to come. As your god, I declare you, MerQueen Aria, shall pardon them," Poseidon said to me, but based on Takar's sigh, he heard it, too.

"Granted," I said as I touched them on the top of their tails before moving back.

I watched in fascination as lights surrounded them before revealing a male and a female, both with striking orange tails that held their mate mark.

I gasped. The fact that a siren had a mate mark, let alone a mate, truly meant they were destined for greatness.

"Raf," I said.

"Yes, your Majesty."

"Please tell everyone to resume. I will be in the royal office with Takar, Cora, Zaz, Lord Titan, and our guests."

"Yes, your Majesty."

"Right this way." I motioned to the door down the hall.

Titan took the lead, and we all headed to the office. Things just got interesting.

Chapter Sixty-Seven

TAKAR

I listened intently as the new mermaids, Oceana and Selas, told their story. It amazed me that there were in fact good sirens out there. From the sound of it, many would join us in our fight against the leaders.

"We will assign you some guards as you travel back and forth to bring us the good ones. Ursa will be among them, and Zaz as well. This will give you a witch and a link to us," Aria said.

"Yes, Your Majesty."

"Now that business is done, please go mingle with your new extended family. Make sure to meet with Sandy as she, too, was once a siren."

They bowed and left, with Cora and Zaz right behind them.

"Well done, Aria. You have made me proud already," Titan said, then left us alone.

"I still have so much to learn," I murmured, feeling defeated.

I was MerKing, and I was so lost in how to do any of this. Aria swam up to me and placed a calming hand on my chest.

"Takar, you are new to our way of life, our customs. You are learning every day and have only just touched the surface. Just as I had to be taught, so do you. Be proud of what you do know and trust in your mate to fill in the blanks."

She always knew just what to say to soothe my anxiety. And, dammit, if she wasn't always right.

I was sitting, so she positioned herself on my lap and snuggled into me. "You may not be a born mermaid, or born into royal status, but you have done so much for Merkind with what you just did with your old boss. Not to mention what you are doing with your company. That is something none of us could have done. That is all you and your glory."

Without a word, I pulled Aria in for a kiss and moaned when her tongue dove right in.

Soon we were upright, our tails twisting together. Sex as a mermaid never lasted long, but our bond grew every time and we felt each other's every emotion.

For me, this was making love. As a lion, it was a hard pounding and as humans, we had both.

I felt myself getting close, and I deepened our kiss. Our tails tightened even more as our moans grew louder.

"Slash," she cried out as I felt her open up, my own release rushing over me. As we both came down, our tails loosened but didn't release. We embraced our love for several minutes. Honestly, I wanted to stay like this forever but we had places to be.

"Let's go back to the party." I unwrapped my tail, grabbed her hand and turned to go.

Chapter Sixty-Eight

ARIA

The celebration was still in full swing, and our new members were fitting right in. Our guard rejoined us as we entered the room.

Ursa smiled at me. "I see you are sending me on a task already."

"Of course. I wouldn't have anyone else go. You are good at what you do."

"Well, I'm flattered, but I will miss you terribly."

I pulled her into a hug. "I will miss you, too. But you know you can reach me whenever," I said, pointing to my head. She smiled.

"Oh, I know."

THE NEXT SEVERAL months were normal. Sirens came under Ursa's blessing, and we granted them asylum and turned into their mermaid forms.

Most were strong warriors and were put to work in the military immediately. My belly was definitely showing, and I was exhausted. I only had two months left, so we knew the fight would reach us soon.

We were past dreading it and were prepared for it in every way. Well, as prepared as you can be for a lot of unknowns.

Several clans came to visit and pay their respects, even loaning us some soldiers.

A clan had just arrived, and Titan was smiling broadly.

"Titan, are you good?" I linked.

"This is the clan your mother went to years ago," he replied.

Well, damn.

"Your Majesty, MerQueen Aria, it is a pleasure to meet you. Your mother was a dear friend and is missed. We were sorry to hear of her passing and now your father's as well," the woman at the front said.

"Thank you for coming," I said.

"Anytime, as you are also welcome to visit us as well."

I felt a tug in my mind, and my head spun. I swayed and Cora was quick to catch me. Desperate to make the spinning stop, I closed my eyes and took a deep breath. Within seconds I was carried out of the main hall and into my quarters, the MerDoc at my side looking me over.

My body buzzed and my head pounded. What the hell was happening?

I was faintly aware of Cora telling the MerDoc what happened, but I was unable to speak. Takar's concerned voice filled my mind, but I still couldn't answer. Even my lion was silent. Honestly, I was beginning to panic.

Suddenly, my body jolted, and a yellow glow surrounded me. Everyone jumped back and just watched in shock and terror.

"Mate of a god shall become a goddess to rule all under her

command in the way of justice and peace. The power of the Cherished-child is now granted to you. My son and now my daughter," Poseidon's voice said.

I could tell it went to everyone linked to me.

Before I could blink, the light was gone, and I felt normal. I slowly sat up and looked around to see all my staff with shocked expressions. I replayed the words in my head. "Mate of a god."

"Your mate is my son. I roamed the earth for years with his mother's people. They worship the ground I walked on. I took a bride and Takar came to be, his powers dormant until they were awoken. As his father, I declare him ready to unlock his powers and grant them to you as well, my sweet daughter," Poseidon said, for only me to hear.

Ho. Ly. Shit!

Chapter Sixty-Nine

TAKAR

Holy shit, I am a god.
Not only that, but my father was Poseidon.
Fuck me.

As I got my powers, Poseidon came to me and told me about him and my mom. I had no clue.

My mate's discomfort and pain sliced through me. Even worse, she couldn't answer me. But now I could feel my power and knew even more that we would come out on top of this.

I left my office as soon as I felt Aria's pain and was by her side quickly. My work for the day was done, anyway. She moved into me as I sat beside her.

"Sorry," she murmured.

I pulled back and looked at her. "For what?"

"Scaring you."

I pulled her back into me. "Don't be."

"The guest clan is worried. They want reassurance that you are alright," Bash said.

I wanted to say *fuck off, she needs rest,* but that was not king-like and it definitely wasn't godlike.

Holding her close to me, we swam together and greeted the clan. Relief washed over their faces.

"My apologies, pregnancy can be a doozie," Aria said. I hid my shock at the withholding of her new status, but I didn't question it.

"Completely understandable."

"Please enjoy our amenities. My mate and I are going to retire for the evening," I said.

"Of course, Your Majesties," the female said before turning to enjoy the public area.

"Come on, let's regroup at home with our guard," I said.

"Sounds good," she whispered, her exhaustion evident. I scooped her up and carried her as I swam to our home.

Chapter Seventy

ARIA

Despite the fact that I felt powerful, I was also fucking exhausted.

Ursa was at my side as soon as I was placed on my couch. It was too early for bed, and I didn't want my guard in our room.

"When you are given power, it can take a lot out of you as your body adjusts to its new norm. As a witch, I went through it. You will be extra tired for a few days, today being the worst."

"Thank you," I whispered.

"So, how are we handling this?" Titan asked.

"For now, it doesn't leave this room. This is an upper hand on the Sirens, and we don't need them figuring it out."

"As you wish, my goddess."

I cringed. "Please, no need, only in front of others, and for now even that is Your Majesty."

"Of course."

Poseidon talked to us more and more as the weeks went on. I was due in another month, and I was ready to be human and not shift for a while. Or lie around in lion form, since it was a lot less uncomfortable.

Clans were still visiting since travel took a good amount of time. We had as many sirens as we could find without being detected, so we were ready. With my huge belly, I wondered how I was going to fight. But I quickly brushed it away, remembering the powers I had yet to discover.

The alarm sounded, and mermaids scattered to shelter. Takar was at my side with our guard around us. A group of twelve sirens were coming in hot, weapons at the ready.

"There are many more coming. Don't worry. I am here with you," Poseidon said.

My belly warmed before it glowed. A jolt of electricity shot out, taking out five of them instantly.

What the hell? Did my child just do that?

The remaining seven slowed their approach. I held out my hand, and a cyclone projected from my palm with the precision of a bullet, taking out five more. Damn.

Takar now stood in front of me, his protective side unable to help himself.

The ocean moved, and I knew without a doubt Takar was the reason.

"How dare you come into my home and try to attack my mate! You will pay dearly for that." His voice sent chills down my spine. There was no mistaking the venom he possessed.

The siren in front smirked, and suddenly there were hundreds of sirens. Which we were expecting. A swift movement from my hands and our army came from what appeared to be out of thin air and attacked.

Screams, tearing, and grunts surrounded us, our guards fighting to keep the sirens away. I smirked when I saw the sharks come to our aid.

Sharks had nothing against mermaids, just sirens. Blood filled the area as sharks took chunks of the enemy. Even Tilly and Willy were doing their part.

I was impressed with how our new members carried themselves, not even fazed by killing the people they grew up with. My lion growled, and I spun around in time to see a siren coming right at me. Takar pushed me out of the way as the knife cut into his chest.

NO!

A cyclone formed around me as my belly glowed again. Bolts of lightning shot through the swirling water. None of my mermaids were affected. The power I felt was exhilarating.

I looked toward Takar and saw he was bleeding. Being underwater, he was unable to shift, so would not heal. The cut was deep, and he looked pale.

"I love you," he linked, his voice weak.

"No, don't die on me. Hang in there," I pleaded. His eyes closed, and I clutched my chest, feeling his presence weaken.

A blue-tailed merman appeared, his hair blue flame, with gold bracelets on his wrists.

Poseidon.

I gasped as he scooped Takar into his arms and shot to the surface. Before I could think, lightning shot out of me and the remaining sirens fell.

My guard and Takar's were on me fast, checking me over. "I'm fine. Takar took the hit."

I wanted nothing more than to go to him, but his father had him, and I had a job to do.

Chapter Seventy-One

TAKAR

The sting of the salt water hurt like a bitch.

I was hit, but my mate was okay. That was all that mattered.

My body went limp as I descended into darkness. I was faintly aware of strong arms around me as I moved quickly.

I was placed down, and a familiar voice demanded, "Shift."

Without hesitation, my lion came forward, and the darkness faded as my lion healed me. I shifted back to my human form and looked to see who had saved me.

I gasped at the man standing before me, his hair a vibrant blue flame, almost like Hades. But I knew it wasn't him.

"Dad," I breathed.

His neutral face turned into a warm smile.

"I never thought I would hear those words from you, son."

He kneeled and scooped me into his arms and just held me. I jerked back.

"Aria," I said, panicking.

"She is safe. The battle is done. Storm did his job, as did his mother."

"Storm?"

"Your son."

My son.

"Your mate is making sure there are no survivors. Her cyclone will only hurt dark souls, good will fall into a slumber. Survivors will be granted asylum and serve some time, but not much. I have spoken to her, and she knows you are with me and safe."

I relaxed a little and turned to my father. "Did my mom know about me, well, you?"

"Yes, she knew I was not of this world, a spirit, if you will. She knew her son was destined for great things. Every person you met was placed there for a reason. Zaz was meant to turn you, Raf to support you, and Aria to teach you."

"Why not raise me?" I asked, immediately feeling bad for interrogating my own father. "Sorry, I—"

"Don't. I owe you many answers, and I will give them all. I know how you hate riddles, so I will try to keep them down."

I chuckled and shook my head. "Riddles are confusing as fuck."

"Indeed, it is to prevent the wrong person from getting the correct information. So it does serve a purpose. Now, to answer your question. Most gods and goddesses can be full of themselves, and I didn't want that for you. I wanted you to be fair and humble, and to accomplish that you had to be kept in the dark."

"Was this part of that plan?" I asked as I motioned to my now-healed wound.

"No, I may be a god, but I am not *the* God. But I was not going to let you die, and that is why Zaz was placed in your path."

Well, damn.

"You resisted your lion and your mate, and I thought I would lose you, but you came around and changed your path from dismay and destruction to powerful and happy."

Chapter Seventy-Two

ARIA

While Takar was with his father, I assisted my soldiers in the search for surviving sirens. Poseidon had told me if they lived, they were good. I was surprised that almost a quarter of the sirens were, in fact, alive.

"Do not fear. Your hearts are not corrupt, so you shall be accepted and spared. Free to live within this clan after you do service."

The group relaxed at my words. They had committed a crime, so they had to be punished. Their basic needs would be provided, and their wages would be held in trust, given to them when they were declared suitable for reentry into society, as a nest egg.

One by one, I touched them, giving them their mermaid form before putting the bracelet of punishment on their wrists. It was similar to handcuffs but spellbound to keep them within a certain location.

The staff was out cleaning the mess, and many soldiers

staying to help as well. I sent a message through the sea that the clans who loaned us warriors could return.

To say I was exhausted was an understatement. I was pregnant, exerted a lot of power and had just gotten my power, so I was famished.

"Aria. Let us bring you to your mate."

I nodded and slumped into Titan's waiting arms.

The journey didn't take long, and Takar was on his feet as soon as we broke the surface, taking me from Titan, who then turned to leave.

Takar laid me between his legs, and I curled into him, resting the best I could.

I opened my eyes and blinked. Muffled voices were talking.

"Hey sleepy," Takar said before running his fingers against my scalp. I looked up and met his gaze.

"I'm sorry, the battle just drained me."

"You exerted a lot of power, which is exhausting enough. Add in the fact you are due in a month and it heightens it."

My head snapped to look to see the god himself, Poseidon. "Hello Aria, nice to meet you."

I sat up and stared at the stunning man in front of me.

Damn, he looked so much like Takar.

"Poseidon," I breathed.

"Yes. Thank you for all you have done for my son. Without you, my seas were doomed to evil, and I could not live with that."

I smiled. "I would do anything for him."

"I know, just as I know you will do anything for Storm."

Who?

Before I could voice the question, Takar pulled me closer to him. "Our son," he whispered, and I gasped, my hand flying to my belly.

Storm.

Chapter Seventy-Three

TAKAR

"**D**ad, as much as I want to ask more questions and truly get to know you, my mate is exhausted and I need to get her home to rest. Tomorrow we will celebrate a job well done as the clan returns with the rest of the clans nearby. Please know you are welcome. You should do the announcement of our status after all," I said.

"Of course, son, I wouldn't miss it for the world. Go tend to your mate. Tomorrow will bring great things."

I didn't have time to think about what that meant.

I lifted my mate and carried her to our home, placing her in the bed, climbing in after her, and letting sleep take me.

WHEN I WOKE, Aria was still asleep in my arms, and I couldn't help but smile. As I went to move, she gripped me tightly and mumbled, "No".

I chuckled at her sudden clinginess. Don't get me wrong, I knew it was because for a moment she thought she'd lost me, so I couldn't blame her. Tonight, after all the duties of the kingdom, I would treat her to a date in the woods on the mainland of my tribe, a few hours from here.

It was sacred and protected by the spirits, so no harm would come to us there, even in our lion forms. We would be seen as gods if caught, which is exactly what we were. Besides, my mom needed to meet her. After the war and my turning, I had never returned home.

A thought hit me. Would my dad want to come and reunite with his old love? Only one way to find out.

"As much as I want to stay in bed with you all day, we have duties to tend to," I said, my voice heavy with sleep.

She squirmed in my arms, and her arousal filled the room. My morning voice always had that effect on her. My chest vibrated with my laughter.

"Hmm, is my Maid horny for her King?"

"Yes," she breathed. In a swift movement, I was out from under her and towering over her.

My lion growled. I knew I needed to take her as a lion, but we didn't have time for that right now.

"How do you want me?" I purred.

"Hard. Fast."

The corner of my mouth moved into a devilish smirk. "With pleasure."

In seconds, we were both naked and my tip was pressed against her entrance. She wrapped her legs around me and desperately tried to pull me in. I held my stance and shook my head.

"Tsk, tsk, tsk, someone woke up feeling slutty today."

"Only for you," she huffed.

That did it. I plunged into her, not stopping until our hips were flush.

Chapter Seventy-Four

ARIA

His cock slid in and I gasped.

Fuck me. Was it possible his cock got even bigger, or was my pregnancy making me feel more full?

"Fuck, Red," he groaned.

I felt his struggle not to cum. Maybe I wasn't mistaken.

He slid out to the tip, then slammed back in.

"Yes," I cried. "Fuck me harder. Fuck me like you own me."

He growled again, then thrust into me over and over. His hands squeezed and pulled my nipples, and I writhed under him. I was fully at his mercy and he knew it.

After all, I almost lost him yesterday, so I was not about to resist my urge to be claimed by my mate.

"I. Love. You. Aria," he grunted with each thrust.

All I could do in response was moan.

"Fucking you speechless, huh?" he growled, and I nodded. "You take my cock so damn good. Now I am going to make you take my cum."

Oh fuck. The threat made my orgasm shoot to the surface,

and I cried out. My body jerked, and his warmth filled me so deep I didn't think it would be leaking out. Damn.

He kissed my mark, sending electricity through me. "Tonight I will claim you again under the stars of my ancestors."

I moaned at the blissful promise.

"Get up and get ready," he said as he slid out his still-hard cock. My eyes bulged, and he looked down. He was, in fact, several inches bigger and even wider than before.

Fuck me.

Chapter Seventy-Five

TAKAR

Well, damn, no wonder she felt so much tighter. I thought it had something to do with our child she was carrying, but no, it was me. I guess when I was given my powers, it also gave a few extra perks. If I had known, I would not have been so rough. She was sure to be sore until she could shift.

When she came out of the bathroom, she moved a little stiffly and slightly bowlegged. I chuckled.

"Shut up," she sneered with very little venom.

"I'm sorry, Maid. If I had known, I would have been easier on you." I pulled her into me. She swatted at my shoulder.

"Nuh-uh. None of that. You know I like it rough. Am I sore? Yes, but we will be in mermaid form, so no worries there."

She had a point.

"True. Okay, I take it back. Maybe next time I will take you even harder."

Her slutty moan told me just how much she liked that idea.

I pinned her to the wall and claimed her lips with mine, taking the kiss I craved as I swallowed her moans of desire. When

I pulled away, I took her hand in mine and walked toward the beach.

Once in the ocean, it didn't take us long to get to the castle. Everyone was waiting there. Well, all the staff and our guards. I looked around and was impressed by the immaculate space. There was no evidence of the fight that almost claimed my life.

Damn, the staff was good.

The MerDoc was the first to speak. "Your Majesties. I am happy to report low casualties. A few will need a few months to recover, but we suffered no lives lost, thanks to you, MerQueen."

I smiled, letting my beautiful mate take her well-deserved praise.

"Please, it wasn't just me. The soldiers and warriors fought valiantly. They, too, deserve credit."

If I were in human form, I would have sprung an erection. She was so damn humble.

"Is the celebration ready?"

"Yes, your Majesty," one of the servants said.

"Council, is there anything we need to tend to today?" I asked.

"No, Your Majesties. As the clans arrive, many will want alliances, but that is tomorrow's issue," Titan answered.

Chapter Seventy-Six

ARIA

I was relieved to find out there were no casualties other than a few wounded. Not even my own mate. Thank the gods.

"Visiting warriors and soldiers. Many of you saw a power radiate from me, and we ask that you refrain from saying too much until the announcement is officially made," I said. I watched as they all bowed their heads in respect and acknowledgement.

Clans began to arrive, and they greeted their loved ones with excitement and gratitude. Each leader thanked me for keeping their warriors safe.

If only they knew.

The castle grounds were filled as much as possible, and everyone was here. Everyone except Poseidon. As if right on cue, he appeared from above in all his glory. Gasps followed by utter silence was all you heard.

"My Merchildren of the sea. It is I, your god Poseidon. The gift of my voice and knowledge has been a part of your

MerQueen's lineage for generations. But now you also have my one and only son, Takar."

Everyone gasped, some with so much force they coughed.

"Your MerKing is a god who lives humbly among you with his mate who, as your warriors witnessed, has her own godly powers granted by me and her unborn son, another god sent to live among all of you. They are the rulers of all rulers in the sea. Listen to them as they create change and better your lives under my guidance."

Everyone cheered, then bowed their respect to the god—well, gods—before them.

Despite the battle and our win, there were more sirens out there. My focus was on finding the good ones and bringing them home to our growing clan.

Poseidon clapped his hands, and a jolt of power surged. I watched in amazement as several mermaids simultaneously found their mates.

My eyes wandered to the god, and he smiled. "I blocked pairings, wanting my children to truly bond and enjoy their mates without impending doom looming over them," he said, answering my unspoken question.

Well, damn.

I gasped as I noticed Titan with the woman from my mom's old chosen clan. A smile spread across my lips. He deserved this 100%.

Chapter Seventy-Seven

TAKAR

The celebration was long, and so many enjoyed the company of my father. I still couldn't believe the god Poseidon was my dad.

"Let's go, I have a surprise for you," I whispered in Aria's ear. Slash practically jumped out of me with excitement at what we were about to do.

We slipped away, my father giving me a knowing wink as we passed. I shook my head and continued.

"I will be there later this evening," he said in my mind, and I smiled.

Once on the mainland, I headed to my land home. We didn't use it, but I kept it just in case we needed it for anything. Aria climbed in the car, and I could feel her nervous energy.

"What is it, Aria?"

"My mom, she was killed by a drunk driver."

Shit, I forgot about that.

"I won't let anything happen to you," I promised as I placed my hand on her thigh. Her body's response was immediate, and a calmness washed over her.

I never moved my hand the whole drive. Every chance I could, I glanced at her as she watched the city turn into the woods. After several hours, we arrived at my mom's place. I got out of the car and opened her door.

As I took her hand in mine, my mom came out with a smile on her face.

"Takar," she exclaimed. "My sweet boy, who is the fine woman beside you?"

"Mom, this is my fiance, Aria."

She beamed, then swatted me on the arm. "You disappear after you came home, then you reappear with a very pregnant almost wife," she scolded.

"Sorry, Mom. I was a mess in the head. But then I met this fine woman, and she helped me find myself in every way possible."

"So why aren't you married to her yet?"

"I-um."

Shit, how did I answer this?

"We have had tons going on, and he had a lot to work through. I didn't want to rush him," Aria said, saving me.

"Aren't you mates?"

My jaw dropped. "Wh-what?"

"You have an aura around you, one only given by the spirits and the gods. One your father possessed."

Holy shit.

"Your father was a god, and I was tasked to carry you. He ran from my love, but I still got you."

I looked at Aria, and she nodded at my unspoken question. I told my mom everything from being turned into a lion, meeting Aria, and everything in between. Including my father.

"My love, how is he?" she asked as I spotted my father coming around the house.

"Why don't you ask him yourself?"

She turned to see what my eyes were focused on. She gasped and her legs gave out. My father was quick to catch her.

"I'm sorry, my beautiful flower. I never should have run from you, from our love. Please forgive me and take me back."

"Finally," she breathed as she pulled him into a deep kiss.

We looked away to give them privacy. "Tomorrow, you two will be married in the human world, no ifs, ands, or buts about it," Posiden said.

"If I may. I would like to not be pregnant," Aria said.

My mom sighed. "Okay. I can understand that."

"How about we get married tomorrow? I kept you waiting long enough," my dad said.

Well, damn.

My mom beamed. "Really?"

"Yes."

"I accept."

We all hung out and talked, and I turned to my mom. "Mom, is the field still safe?"

"If you are asking if the field is still protected and able to accommodate your lions, the answer is yes. We have an ally staying in the woods. He is friendly, so don't be alarmed if you run into him."

"Oh," I said, raising an eyebrow.

"He is like you—well, not a lion, but a shifter. His animal is the tiger."

Interesting.

"His name is Rajayah. He is here to find his mate among our people. Many are off to school, so this summer we hope he finds her."

"Looks like we have to make friends before we can enjoy the night sky," Aria linked.

"I guess we do."

Chapter Seventy-Eight

ARIA

As soon as his mom saw Poseidon, I felt and saw the love radiating off them. Now we were walking to the woods to let our lions free and, apparently, meet another shifter.

Part of me wondered if Poseidon would live here or how all that would work, and also why another non-North-America-based shifter resided in this area.

We entered a field, and I looked around. The sound of twigs snapping had us both looking over to the right. A man came into view in nothing but basketball shorts. He didn't seem nervous at the pair of us.

"You must be Rajayah," Takar said.

"I am. Who might you be?"

"I am Takar, son of Poseidon. My mom said you were here."

"Your mother."

"Hopi, like the tribe," Takar said, and the man visibly relaxed.

"She said her son never came home after his service."

"I needed time to find myself."

He nodded like he understood. "I served for years in the Army, went to many battles. I know how lost one can get. Hell, I still am. Your father sent me a message about my mate being here, so now here I am," he said. I watched as a lightbulb seemed to go off. "Wait, you are Poseidon's son, so are you a god?"

"Yes," Takar replied. Rajayah's bow was immediate. "Please, no need. And don't call me god, or anything. Just Takar."

"Of course. Please call me Raj."

"What is your tiger's name?"

"You will laugh."

"Try me," Takar said.

"Rajiv."

"No, not funny, just ironic, like mine and my mates. My lion's name is Slash and my mate's lion's name is Red." He quirked an eyebrow. "When I was turning, I was in a war zone and had been attacked. People would question if I stayed uninjured, if I were to go missing as long as I was. So I was turned but only allowed to heal enough not to die, leaving me with scars. As for my mate, well, her hair is a vibrant red."

"Well damn. I was just about to go into town and get a few things. I would love to prepare you a meal in my little cabin later. But I will leave you for now. Please enjoy the woods and all it has to offer," he said, then gave a slight bow before leaving us.

I turned to my mate. "He seemed nice."

"Yes, yes, he did."

Chapter Seventy-Nine

TAKAR

"My goddess. This land is sacred and safe for us to shift in. Even if seen, the tribe will only worship us. The kids may try to climb us, but that is all."

"Hmm. Shifting sounds nice."

"Then shift."

She took a step back before shifting. Her lion shook out all the kinks from being confined.

Don't get us wrong, we shifted at home, but lately we have been mermaids or human.

I shifted next, and Slash immediately rubbed all over her, marking her with his scent as he nipped and licked her. I stayed back, letting him have his moment, and felt Aria doing the same for Red.

Red pounced on a bunny as it hopped by and ate it whole, blood dripping from her jaw.

Fuck, that was hot.

Slash moved toward her and licked her jaw clean. I moved back, letting him take full control and have his mate.

Once he was done, I came forward and lay down next to my mate as we looked at the sky. The sunset was stunning against the treeline, and I found myself at peace. Not only that, but more at peace than I have ever been in my life.

Rustling came from slightly behind me, so I lifted my head and turned. I relaxed when I saw it was Rajayah.

"My apologies," he said.

I shook my head and gently stood before shifting and sitting down, placing my mate's head in my lap.

"Nah, don't be. She is very pregnant, and the day has been long."

"Of course. I will get started on dinner. Um, do you have any requests?"

"No Rajiv. But after dinner, may we see your animal?"

"It would be an honor."

Instead of shifting back, I sat with my mate curled in my lap and stroked her soft fur. This would never get old in any way, and soon we would have a child to add to our crazy life.

Storm.

I smiled, knowing just what my little boy was capable of already. The three of us would be unstoppable.

The aroma of whatever Rajiv was cooking surrounded us, and Red stirred. She lifted her head and took a deep sniff. I stroked her between the ears.

"Rajiv is cooking for us," I whispered into her ear.

She rubbed her face against me, then stood up, shifting into her human form before sitting between my legs. "Well, it smells fantastic, and even Storm is interested."

I chuckled and rubbed her back. "Between the two of you, you could eat a whole grocery store."

"Are you calling me fat?" she retorted.

"Heavens no. You are drop-dead gorgeous and in no way fat."

She smirked, then pulled me into a kiss. I could hear the footsteps approaching, but I was so damn lost in my mate that I didn't care. I just assumed it was Rajiv.

A loud roar had me shifting and standing over my still-human mate. I was stunned stupid as I saw Rajiv fighting a wolf. Not just any wolf, but a shifter.

What the hell?

"Shift and go to my mom's, send my dad," I linked.

Aria nodded and took off, shifting in mid-stride.

Rajiv was doing fairly well, but I wanted this over quickly. Cats and dogs were notorious for being enemies, but I would not stand for this. I waited for just the right moment, then pounced on the wolf, pinning him down easily. I snarled at their throat, daring them to move. The wolf tilted his head and shifted to human, and I followed suit. Rajiv was also now human.

"Rajiv, what happened?" I asked.

"He came through the woods and was heading to you, his head low like he was stalking his prey. You were, um, distracted, so I did what I needed to in order to keep my god safe."

Damn.

I felt proud. Not only did a shifter I barely knew come to my and my mate's defense, he considered me his god.

"G-god?" The man pinned beneath me stammered. I looked down at him and smirked.

"I am the son of Poseidon," I snarled. "And you just attempted to kill me and my mate, an act punishable by death."

The scent of fear was strong enough to make me want to gag. The sound of hurried steps behind me told me my mate and my dad were here. Red walked up to me, still in lion form, my father on her back like she was a horse.

Part of me balked at that, but it was faster than just running as humans.

As long as my mate and Storm were okay, I was fine with it, and my dad wouldn't do anything to harm our child.

My dad slid down and scratched Red between the ears.

"What seems to be the problem?" Poseidon asked.

"This wolf shifter tried to attack me and my mate," I snarled, never breaking eye contact with the man below me. My dad placed his hand on my back, and I stood up, my eyes daring the man to get up.

"Explain yourself," Poseidon ordered.

"I was ordered by my alpha to prevent the child's birth."

My body heated with anger. He was trying to kill my son.

Slash tried to push forward, but I held him back, though it was not easy. Red pressed herself against me, and I leaned into her. Her love and comfort relaxed me instantly.

"Who is your alpha?"

"Zion," he replied.

"What is your name?"

"Adam."

"Adam, your soul is good, and you received an order. For that, your life will be spared. Your ties to that pack end today, when your mate comes through the trees, but you are to lure your Alpha here. You are to tell him you have Aria hostage, and he can kill her himself."

He nodded and did what he was told. Now we waited.

"I made enough food for everyone, so please enjoy it while we wait," Rajiv said.

"Indeed, it smells delicious," Aria said as she shifted back into her human form.

Chapter Eighty

ARIA

After Takar made sure I had enough food and was between him and his father, he got his plate. The salmon, green beans, and potatoes were absolutely delicious. Whatever the sauce on them, it was unlike anything I had ever experienced before.

I was still tense about the wolf eating with us, but Poseidon could see his soul and, despite his attempt on my life, he was good.

"The Alpha order is undeniable and hard to fight, especially by a low-ranking wolf like Adam," Poseidon said.

Suddenly my lion rushed forward, and I was up and in my lion form in seconds. Takar was right behind. Rajiv, now a tiger, stood in front of me as well.

Who would have thought a tiger and a lion would get along, let alone protect each other?

A black wolf appeared, his eyes flickering with anger. He took in the scene before him. Not only were there two lions, a tiger, and a tall man with fierce blue hair, but his own wolf was standing confidently next to the man.

Slash looked at Rajiv, who nodded. In seconds, Takar was human and next to his father.

"You dare order my child killed," Takar sneered.

"Your child doesn't belong among us."

"Do you know who I am?" Poseidon asked.

"I don't give a damn who the fuck you are. You are of no importance to me," he spat.

Oh shit. Big mistake.

"Oh, but that is where you are mistaken, pup. I am not someone to mess with, and neither are my son and his mate. Your soul is corrupt and filled with evil. I declare your status stripped from you, and you will live out your life confined in a cell."

"You have no right."

"Oh yes, I do. I am Poseidon, and the Moon Goddess is on her way to deal with you."

His eyes widened comically, and I couldn't help but smirk.

I shifted to human form as a woman in white appeared.

"My pup, why have you disgraced us?" the woman said. "Shifters, whether of the moon or the sun, are sacred. You attempted to kill one of your own using a pawn. Not only that, but you tried to kill my nephew before his time on earth. Poseidon's punishment is fair and just. I hereby strip you of your title, and I will personally hold you in a cell."

She turned to look at the man standing next to Poseidon. "Adam, I deem you the new Alpha."

As soon as the words were spoken, he shifted into a wolf, which was now bigger. His aura was evident.

Damn.

"You are connected to Aria, Rajayah, Takar, myself, and Poseidon. Your mind can link no matter the distance. Now wait here and your mate will appear. Claim her, she will accept you, then go to your pack and take what is yours."

He stood tall over the previous alpha, now small, lying at the goddess's feet.

"And you, my shifter Rajayah. You are a servant of the god Takar and the goddess Aria, and you, too, will be connected to them. Be ready. Your mate is coming this way soon. She has her own journey to fulfill before she is ready for you."

Chapter Eighty-One

TAKAR

The moon goddess was stunning, to say the least, and I was awestruck. A woman walked into the field, and Adam's reaction was instant. All of us headed into the woods to give them privacy, the moon goddess disappearing with the defeated wolf.

I wished she could have stayed, but I understood she had things to do.

"Rajiv, thank you for what you did," I said.

"Haikuwa shida, kwa kweli."

I gasped at the use of Swahili. My mom was originally from Africa on her mom's side, her father, Native American.

"What did he say?" Aria linked me.

"It was no problem, really," I replied.

"Hata kidogo. Una shukrani yangu," I said in response to him, while Slash translated to Aria.

"Rajiv, you have a room at mine and my partner's home. Takar and Aria, there is a guesthouse down the road that you are welcome to," Poseidon said.

I turned to Aria and pulled her to me. "Shall we?"

"Yes," she breathed. Then we headed to the guesthouse. There was no way we were going home just to come back.

"Raf, bring the guard tomorrow. Titan can hold down the fort. My mom is getting married, and we had an incident today, so it is better to be safe than sorry," I linked.

"Copy that, and I will need all the information on what the hell you mean and how all of a sudden your mom is getting married."

I let Slash take over and fill him in while I took care of my other need, the need to fuck the hell out of my mate.

"Bed now," I ordered as soon as we were in the door.

She whimpered and scurried down the hall into the single bedroom. I stalked behind her, licking my lips, knowing just what I planned to do to her. I smiled devilishly when she started losing her clothes on the way.

As soon as she was on the bed, I pounced until my tongue was inside her leaking folds. I swirled my tongue as she gripped the sheets.

"Fuck," she huffed.

"Hmm. So damn sweet," I purred.

Her pregnancy made her ultrasensitive, and now I was even bigger in the cock department, so I wanted her to be nice and wet. I ran my hand up her body until I held her breasts in my hands.

Damn, they were definitely getting bigger. The realization made my cock leak.

"Hmm. I am going to love it when these beautiful mounds get even bigger."

"Fuck me," she begged.

"Such a needy Maid." I moved up her body, lining my cock just right to take her.

Slash warred in my mind for control, and I slammed into her, making her take me all at once. Her eyes rolled back as she moaned. Her legs wrapped around me as I pulled back out before slamming back in.

"Oh god," she cried out.

"Yes, I am a god. I am your god. You, my goddess, take my cock so damn good." My tone was some kind of growl, grunt, and I don't even know what, but fuck if it didn't seem to turn her on even more. She hadn't even cum yet and already we were covered in fluids.

Fuck me. I was about to lose my load, but I wouldn't let her off that easy. No, she was going to take my cock over and over again until it was time for the wedding or I needed a break.

Whichever came first.

"I am going to fill your tight little hole. Then I am going to flip you onto your hands and knees and fill you again, and only then can you cum," I ordered.

"Yes, my King, my god," she moaned.

My hips jolted as my first jet of cum shot from my cock. The feeling of her body fighting to disobey my command made my eyes roll with pleasure.

"Your body drives me crazy," I growled.

Once I knew she had taken every last drop, I pulled out of her and guided her to flip over. Her ass was teasing me, my cock already prepared for round two. I gripped her cheeks and bent down to lick her from front to back.

I lined myself up and slowly slid in. She circled her hips, and I groaned before swatting her ass.

"Easy there, Maid. This is my show."

She whimpered, and I slid out before roughly plunging back in. My balls were already drawing up with my next release. I gripped her hair and braced myself against her hips.

"So. Damn. Good."

My hand left her hair and moved to her throat as I added pressure while yanking her up into me. Her walls spasmed, and I knew she desperately needed to fall.

"Cum now," I ordered.

Chapter Eighty-Two

ARIA

As soon as the words left his mouth, I collapsed onto the bed as my body convulsed with my orgasm, his seed filling me again as he roared out his release.

Fuck, that would never get old.

My body was exhausted, and I sank into the mattress. Takar fell right beside me.

I woke up to Takar resting his hand on my belly as he laid soft kisses on my baby bump. The love he already had for our child was visible.

"Looks like Mommy is awake. Bonding time is over for now, little man," he whispered.

My lips turned up into a smile. Takar's eyes lifted from my

belly to mine, making my breathing hitch at the amount of love and hunger in his eyes.

Oh fuck.

There was no doubt about what was about to happen, and my body responded.

I squirmed as he crawled over me, kissing me all the way up my body, stopping at my breasts and nipping my tender nipples.

"Fuck," I breathed.

"Hmm, Maid, you are so damn responsive to me, so sensitive to my touch. And so damn sexy while you carry our child. Just looking at you is enough to make me explode." He moved the rest of the way up my body until his lips were on mine. I moaned into his mouth as his hand cupped my dripping pussy. "Hmm. I am going to fuck you, then we have a wedding to get to."

Oh god.

"Yes," I gasped as his finger pushed inside me.

I could feel myself getting wetter and, honestly, I was pretty sure the bed was soaked already. In the last couple of weeks, I had been ultrasensitive, and it only seemed to get worse every day.

My back arched as he pressed his tip just inside me. I reached for his arms, desperately begging for more. I wanted him inside me. He let out a long moan as he slowly slid his cock deep into my core.

Wanting more friction, I circled my hips. He growled and braced his arms around my head. His eyes bored into me as he moved his hips back until he was almost out of me. A smirk that looked like it should only be worn by the devil spread across his lips before he slammed into me so hard I thought I would cum right then and there.

Oh fuck.

His thrusts were punishing, and I loved every second of it.

Our gazes never left each other, neither of us closing our eyes. As rough and hard as he was pounding me in every way, this was making love.

Euphoria spread across his face and his eyes rolled. He was getting close, and just the thought of him filling me with his seed was enough to bring my orgasm to the surface.

"I'm about to——"

My release exploded from my core. I cried out as my body twitched and writhed. Takar growled as his cock jerked with his first jet of cum. The warmth of his seed made me moan all over again.

"Moan like that again and we might just miss the wedding," he growled in a whisper.

Oh fuck.

Chapter Eighty-Three

TAKAR

Hearing my mate moan after the pounding I just gave her made me want to take her all over again, but I was not about to miss my parents getting married. But as soon as we got home, it would be on. All night long.

And that was a promise.

Despite my half-hard erection, we arrived at my mom's place in time for the wedding. Aria stayed with my mom while I went to assist my father in getting ready.

"Hey Dad." I walked in the door of the spare room.

Rajiv was also there, and he bowed slightly.

"I was just about to go make sure everything outside was ready," he said as he left the room.

Part of me was upset that someone other than me was helping my dad get ready, but I hadn't exactly been here. Though I also knew Raj was a guest in this house and had offered to help, so I couldn't complain.

"Son, I am so glad you are here. I'm a damn mess," my dad said.

I raised an eyebrow as I tied his tie around my neck so I could just slip it on once he was dressed.

"Why? You love her, right?"

"There is no doubt about that, Takar."

"Then what's the problem?" I asked, genuinely confused. He motioned for me to take a seat next to him, so I did.

"Like shifters, gods have a way of marriage outside of the human world. A shifter has a bite, mermaids have sex in their natural form. And a god brands their mate with their symbol. To a human, it will look like a tattoo, but it's more than that. When you fully awaken as a god, you mark your bride too. The night we conceived you, I bred your mom, but I never marked her. I wanted to. Gods, I wanted to, but my father wouldn't allow me to claim a human. I refused to claim a god or any other immortal, so his powers faded and I was unmated. I saved myself for her, never having sex again. This wedding means that tonight she will be branded by me after almost thirty years. I'm nervous."

"Don't be. My mom waited for you too. She never lay with another man. She raised me and taught me everything I know. Even when I left for the military, she just focused on helping others and preserving the land. She never even looked twice at another man. She always said her soulmate would return. And now here you are. My mom fucking loves you, always has, always will."

He took a deep breath and visibly relaxed.

"I'm assuming my mom knows what happens next?" I asked.

"Yes. I told her last night."

"Good. Then I see no problems."

"I see the amazing job she did with you, son. I only wish I could have helped her more," he said.

"More?"

He smiled. "Yeah, I may not have been here, but I made sure you had what you needed, made a visit or two to your teacher, who was sworn to secrecy. I just wish you could have known me, that I could have been more hands-on."

"Dad, don't go there. You can't change the past, but you can be here now, and be here for Storm. Teach all of us how to use our powers and do right as gods."

He huffed a laugh as if he had an unspoken joke, or maybe a memory. I patted his shoulder, then slipped the tie over his head and secured it in place.

"Now, enough sappy shit. Go marry the love of your life."

Chapter Eighty-Four

ARIA

I walked into my mother-in-law's room and she beamed. "Am I glad to see you," she sighed.

"Is there a problem?"

"I'm nervous. I waited so long for this, and now I am a damn mess."

"Your love survived almost thirty years. You both deserve this. Not to mention, in case you forgot, sex with a god is mind-blowing."

Her eyes widened at my comment, then she smiled. "I mean, it's been thirty years, but yeah, I do remember that."

I walked up to her and slid her dress over her head before turning her to face me. "To think now you can have it whenever you want, and there is no doubt he would ever refuse you," I whispered in her ear. She gasped and pulled back.

"Does my son ever leave you alone?"

I laughed. "Yeah, sometimes, though not often, but it goes both ways. The only time he refuses is when we have to do something, but even then sometimes I get him to cave and the other way around too."

"Oh joy, well hopefully, Poseidon can keep his hands off me long enough to meet my grandchild and see my son get married."

"Maybe just enough, but right before and right after is fair game," I said through laughter. She rolled her eyes.

"Thank you, dear. I always wanted a daughter, and now I have that and so much more," she said as she placed her hand on my belly. I smiled and pulled her into a hug.

"Enough sappy shit. Let's finish up so you can get married and enjoy the love of your life."

"Yes, let's," she said, settling down into her chair so I could finish up her look. I spun her around and looked her in the eyes.

"He is going to fight not to devour you in front of everyone. You look like a goddess. Well, I mean, you will be soon enough."

Chapter Eighty-Five

TAKAR

My dad's expression of pure love when he saw my mom coming down the aisle was priceless. I hated it took so long for them to be together, but was thankful to have been a part of their union.

My mom made a beautiful bride, and I had to tap the back of my dad's head when he started thinking nasty thoughts. He had been so entranced he didn't realize our link was open.

Needless to say, I didn't want to be anywhere near here when their honeymoon officially started. The whole tribe was here and a few friends. We met everyone and did some dancing with our parents.

I could feel Aria's exhaustion. It was time to go. I walked up to my parents, who were still eating some cake. "Mom, Dad. My mate is exhausted. I am going to take her back to our home."

"Of course," my mom beamed.

"We will visit soon," my dad said.

"After I find my mate. I would love to meet the rest of your pride," Rajiv said, coming up behind me.

"Of course. I would have it no other way."

After a few more goodbyes, we headed home. Aria fell asleep in the car, and I drove in silence.

The ride was peaceful. Being on the road had always been relaxing. Knowing how Aria's mom passed, I never asked her to go on a drive with me. This was the first time, but with my business, I would need to travel and that included driving. I just hoped she would come with me on some of those trips.

"Ursa," I linked as I pulled into my mainland home.

"Yes," she asked.

"Aria is sleeping. Can you transport us home, or should I just take her inside?"

"Take her inside. I'm not comfortable with a transport spell with her being this pregnant. We are on the way to keep guard."

"Okay, sounds good." I shut off the link and carried my sleeping mate into my home and laid her gently on the bed. I fetched some snacks and brought them into the room in case she woke up hungry.

The front door opened, and I left the room. I looked down the stairs and smiled at Zaz and the rest of the guard. "Please make yourselves comfortable. I will be in bed with my mate."

Everyone nodded, and I headed back into the room, my own fatigue making itself known. My breath caught at the sight of Aria in my old bed. She looked so peaceful. Soon she would be my wife, and I would have her in every way.

Chapter Eighty-Six

ARIA

It had been a few days since the wedding, and I was still exhausted. We managed to leave and go to the island, but I have been human ever since. Storm was due any day, and we were ecstatic. I was also nervous as hell. Titan was doing everything from the business to the immediate needs at the castle. The staff had been amazing and accommodating.

I hated how tired I was. I didn't even have the energy to do more than give Takar a blowjob, and that took everything out of me.

Fuck me.

I wanted him so damn bad, but my body said no. After I had Storm, I would be busy with a newborn, so fucking would take a back seat.

Takar was talking to Zaz down the hall, and I was lying down. I hurt all over and, my back was screaming at me. Honestly, I was so over being pregnant.

As soon as I laid down, I felt a pop, then wetness between my legs.

What the?

I looked down and saw the clear fluid.

Did I just pee myself or…?

The thought was cut off as my stomach tightened. I screamed out in pain, and Takar was by my side in seconds with Ursa.

"Her water broke," Ursa said.

Takar lifted me from the bed and carried me to the oversized tub. Cora already had the water going. Water births supposedly helped humans with pain and ease, and if Storm came out in mermaid form, it was ideal.

Another contraction hit, and I whimpered in Takar's chest. He was in nothing but shorts, sitting behind me and holding me to him.

"Breathe, you got this," he whispered into my ear.

"It hurts," I whined.

"I know, love. Soon it will be over. Just breathe and do your best to relax."

I nodded as I sank further back into him as his hands rubbed me.

Honestly, I didn't know if I could do this without him.

Chapter Eighty-Seven

TAKAR

Zaz and the guys were all outside, standing guard. Zaz had already sent word to my parents and Titan.

Now it was a waiting game.

I hated seeing Aria in so much pain, and I wanted desperately to take it all from her, but all I could do was to be here and support her.

Ursa checked, and she was still seven centimeters dilated, where she had been for the last several hours.

I looked up when my mom came in the door.

Thank god.

My mom was a midwife for the tribe, and she would know just what to do to get my mate's labor unstalled.

"Mom, am I glad to see you," I said.

"How is she?" she asked as she kneeled next to the tub.

"She stalled at seven."

"Ah, I see. That's an easy fix," my mom said, taking Aria's hand. She pressed down on a few spots, and Aria cried out as another contraction hit.

Her contractions suddenly seemed longer and more frequent as my mom worked her body over with pressure points. I assumed it was acupuncture or something to that effect.

Ursa moved to check again and smiled. "Time to push," she said.

Thank the heavens.

Chapter Eighty-Eight

ARIA

The pain was intense. Takar was doing everything in his power to keep me comfortable, and I appreciated it fully.

I was ready for this baby to get the hell out.

When Mom came, I was so damn relieved. The next thing I knew, it was time to push.

"Aria, when your next contraction hits, I need you to push with everything you have until the contraction lets up."

I nodded and felt my muscles tighten with my contraction. I did as I was told and collapsed back into Takar's arms.

"You got this," he whispered into my ear as he continued to massage my body. I was tired and didn't know how much more I could take.

"Is he out yet?" I pleaded.

"Not yet. He is crowning. A few more good pushes and you will officially be parents," Ursa said.

I groaned as another contraction hit. Sure enough, after a few more pushes, his shoulders were out, and he practically slid out.

"Human," Ursa said, and I smiled.

Storm was placed in my arms, and I couldn't help the tears that fell. He was so damn beautiful. His hair was a stunning gray, fitting his name.

So precious.

After I delivered my placenta, everyone left the room, leaving Takar and me alone with our son. Tomorrow, we would make the official announcement.

Everything was ready, so now the last-minute stuff needed to get done. Then we would shift and go to the castle.

I was mesmerized as he fed from me, the little noises making me giggle.

Damn. I made this. With help, of course.

"Aria, we should shift so you can heal faster," Takar murmured into my temple as he placed a kiss there.

"How do we teach him to shift?"

"Same way I taught you."

With Takar's help, I got up and out of the tub and outside to the field. He shifted first, and I laid Storm down and shifted. The pain relief was instant, and though I was tired, I was healed physically.

Now all I needed was a good nap. Though Storm might make that difficult.

Takar commanded the shift, and I watched in utter shock as my baby shifted into a small, pure white lion.

Holy shit.

Takar seemed just as shocked as I was. When I looked back, Storm was trying to stand up. I walked over and guided him until he was standing. I laughed when he stumbled and face-planted but was quick to help him back up.

Within minutes he was running around the field, with the occasional somersault and wipeout. He would be the most dependent in human form, so we would save that for being in public on land and sleep. But the days he would spend as a mermaid or a lion.

"Lay down and get some sleep, I'll let him get his energy out," Takar said, and I curled up, closing my eyes to the sight of Takar pouncing around teasing our son.

Chapter Eighty-Nine

TAKAR

When I saw that Storm was white, my mind immediately flooded with questions. The main one was why?

That was a question for my father when he came in the morning.

Red was asleep after being in labor for twenty-four hours. I played and taught Storm how to live as a lion. Hearing his voice in my head was amazing. It was getting late, and we needed to go home and sleep.

Almost like Storm sensed it, he ran over to his still-sleeping mom and pounced on her, biting her like he was going to do some damage.

She lifted her head and swatted him, sending him rolling off her body. She pulled him to her and licked him before standing and shaking off her fur.

"Okay, little rascal, I'm awake, but it is now bedtime," she said, then shifted. Storm whined, but I gave him a look and he jumped into Aria's arms before shifting back to human. I shifted and wrapped my arm around my stunning mate.

Looking at her, you never would have thought she'd just had a baby. Fucking stunning.

We headed inside, and after a quick feeding for Storm, we put him in his crib.

"Go sit in bed. I'll bring you some food," I said as I placed my lips on hers. She yawned, then headed to the room.

I pulled the meatloaf, green beans, and potatoes Zaz cooked earlier and made us each a plate. Storm was peacefully asleep as I walked past his room.

We had talked about him sleeping in our room, but with our sex drives, we determined it was a bad idea.

Aria smiled warmly as I entered the room. I pulled out the trays and placed hers in front of her, then took my own seat. Clearly she was hungry because I swear that food was gone in two seconds. Damn.

"Hungry much?" I asked with my mouth full.

"Not just for food," she said. I swallowed thickly as I noticed the desire in her eyes.

Oh fuck.

Thankfully, unlike humans, gods and mermaids aren't fertile right after having a child. So sex was safe and not risky in any way.

But damn, that was fast.

No longer hungry for the last of my food, I pushed my tray to the side, and my beautiful mate wasted no time in straddling me. I gripped her hips and groaned as she ground herself against me.

Fuck me.

"I need your cock deep inside me," she moaned against my neck. My cock twitched and in seconds, I had her flipped under me.

"Oh, do you now?" I growled, making her whimper and squirm beneath me.

"Yes," she hissed.

"And just how do you want it, hmm?" I jabbed my tip into her thigh.

"Hard."

With pleasure.

"Hmm, I am going to ram my cock so deep you feel me even after we are done. Then I am going to fill you with my seed while I choke you. Next, I am going to make you squirt all over me twice before I let you sleep."

Chapter Ninety

ARIA

Oh fuck.

The things this man wanted to do to me were sinful, and I fucking loved it.

Don't get me wrong, we had plenty of sex while I was pregnant, but my belly did make some things harder to achieve, so I was ready for it all.

"Yes," I breathed. His tip pressed against my opening, and I moaned long and deep as he slid into me. We both wanted it rough and hard, but I did just have a baby, so I didn't mind him playing it safe before cranking it up a notch.

"Fuck, Maid. I think you are tighter than before," he said through gritted teeth, as if he was trying not to cum already. He felt so damn good inside me. All I could do was moan.

He glided back before thrusting back in. It was hard, but not hard enough.

"Harder," I begged.

The growl he let out sent a shiver down my spine. I looked

into his eyes as he pulled his hips back again. I gasped as all I saw was feral, uncaged lust. Poseidon have mercy on my pussy.

Wait, ew, forget that.

Gods have mercy on my pussy.

That's better.

Pleasure shot through my system as he rammed his length into me, his tip almost seeming to hit my chest. I cried out as he did it over and over again. My body shook, and I felt like I would explode from the amount of pleasure coursing through me.

He was definitely going to leave bruises, and I relished it. I wouldn't shift to heal. No, I wanted to feel this.

His hips never lost momentum as he roamed my body with his hands, stopping at my engorged breasts. I needed to feed Storm soon.

He gave an evil smirk before bending down and biting my nipple before sucking.

Relief washed over me as a small amount of liquid escaped my nipple, coating his tongue. He moved his mouth to mine, allowing me a taste as well.

Fuck, that's sweet.

I could feel he wanted more but was glad he resisted.

Our baby needed it, but a small taste was fine by me.

His hand continued up my body until his fingers were wrapped around my neck. He added just enough pressure to send my body into overdrive.

I was nearing orgasm and, based on his erratic movements, so was he.

I dug my nails into his shoulder, and he growled as he slammed into me harder than ever before. His growl turned into a roar as the warmth of his seed filled me. The grip on my neck tightened as his other hand clamped down on my clit. A waterfall of cum exploded from me as I soaked the space between us.

Just as I was coming down, he bit my mark, making a tsunami explode from inside my core. Both of us were coated in my cum.

Damn.

He positioned himself over me, his tip bumping against my lips as his face brushed against my thigh.

Knowing exactly what he wanted, I began to clean myself off of him, moaning as his tongue did the same thing.

He was faster than I was, but I was savoring it. Not to mention he only came once, so I owed him one. I sucked his length, taking all of him at once. He collapsed onto his elbows, and he growled.

"Damn," he moaned.

I hummed against his shaft as I worked my tongue up and down his length. His cock twitched, and I sucked harder, desperate to taste his essence. I cupped his balls and squeezed gently. He roared as the first jet of his cum slammed into the back of my throat. I swallowed against his cock, sucking, making sure to get every last drop.

When I released him, he dove onto the bed, avoiding collapsing on me. I smirked when I saw just how sated he was.

A small cry snapped me back to reality, and I was out of bed. I grunted as the soreness hit. Takar was propped up on his elbow, looking at me with a pleased expression. I couldn't help but roll my eyes.

Fucker.

I flipped him off, then walked stiffly to Storm's room.

<h1 style="text-align:center;">Chapter Ninety-One</h1>

TAKAR

I managed to hold back my laugh as Aria walked like my cock was still buried inside her. Eventually, I gathered enough energy to get up and check on my little family. When I walked into the nursery, Aria was singing softly to Storm as he nursed.

So fucking beautiful.

The sight of my mate with my cub was the best thing I would ever see. I was proud of her. Hell, I was proud of myself. It wasn't long ago that I hated myself and fought against my happiness. Now I was drowning in it.

She looked up and smiled as she seemed to sense my presence. I took the seat next to her on the rocking bench. My arm rested on her shoulder as I looked down at our sleep-eating baby.

Utter perfection.

As soon as he was done and back in his crib, Aria and I headed to our room and let sleep consume us.

I woke up to an empty bed, and I quickly sat up and looked around.

No Aria.

I slipped on my boxers and headed down the hall, sighing in relief when I saw her sitting with an apparently very hungry baby.

"I'm sorry, I didn't hear him. I would have——" I started.

"You don't have to wake up every time, my King. Besides, he didn't cry. I woke up engorged and needed relief, so I came in here. He was awake and looking at the ceiling."

"A mom knows when her baby needs to be fed."

"Exactly."

"I'll go make some breakfast," I mumbled through a yawn.

"I'm pretty sure the parents in our kitchen got that handled."

My eyes widened as I looked down at my barely clothed state, then looked at her and noticed she was in shorts and a sleep top.

I turned and ran to the room and threw on a T-shirt and a pair of sweats.

Once dressed for company, well, okay, maybe dressed for comfort, but at least I had clothes on, I headed to the kitchen and was immediately tackled by my mother.

"Congratulations, Dad," she beamed.

I hugged her back, and my dad came over and gave me a much calmer but just as excited hug.

"How was your first night?" he asked.

"Good, he shifted into his lion. He was a stunning pure white cub," I said.

My dad's eyes grew big before a smile stretched across his lips.

"Well damn. He is going to do great things, son. You must

teach him right. The sirens will return, and he is the key to their undoing."

"Well, hopefully, nothing dangerous. Isn't that what humans say about their kids?" Aria said as she walked into the kitchen with a happy-looking baby in her arms. "I mean, I figure with his abilities and what we are, it will be, but I trust the gods gave him the tools he will need to be triumphant."

"Exactly," my dad said. "Now let me meet my grandchild."

He reached out for Storm. Aria handed him over before coming to my side. The amount of love radiating from my father was suffocating.

"I hope there is enough love for the rest of us," Titan said as he came in the door.

"There will be no fighting over our child," I said sternly.

"Nah, we will leave that for the ladies, or the guys, when he is of age," Zaz said, and I rolled my eyes so hard I thought they would never be normal again.

"Zaz, he is a baby, not a teenager," Aria retorted.

"And?"

"Never mind," she mumbled.

Two plates were placed on the bar, and I helped a still sore Aria into her chair before getting in mine. My dad raised a knowing eyebrow as he handed Storm to Titan. Choosing to ignore him, I dug in.

The morning was spent playing pass the baby. Soon we would head to the beach and have Storm shift into a mermaid so we could introduce the prince to the clan. Then, in a few more weeks, we would be officially married in the human world. As dumb as it sounded, life kept getting in the way. My demon, the death of my mate's father, becoming royalty, finding out I'm a god, my mom, the birth of our child. We had forgotten about our human side, but that ended soon.

I would be lying if I said I wasn't nervous, though I had no clue why.

In the lion world we were married, and in the mermaid world and hell, even in the god world, well minus a mark that I would give her soon. My dad had said we needed to have a child first before I was granted one.

I would give that to her on our wedding night.

Chapter Ninety-Two

ARIA

Storm seemed to soak up all the attention, and there was
definitely no shortage of it.

We got to the beach, and I shifted into my mermaid form
while holding Storm in my arms.

"Shift like Mommy did," I said.

In seconds, I was holding a white cub, and I let out a laugh.
"No, no. We have to swim so we need our fins. See, look at
Mommy's." I flicked my tail up, still holding him securely.

I could see the look of concentration, then watched as his
pure white fin appeared. I gasped, and so did everyone else.

He was pure beauty.

Takar shifted, and then everyone followed as I moved us
under the surface. Once fully under, I let go of Storm and
watched as he flipped upside down.

He giggled and flicked his tail, trying to find his balance,
which only made him spin.

I grabbed his hand and held him upright as I pointed to the

muscles he needed to use, then at his dad. From there, it only took a few tries, and he had it.

"Good, now we have to swim. Stay close, and if you get tired, one of us will carry you," I said.

He took off, and we had to jet ahead to catch him. Little bugger was fast.

As we neared the castle grounds, I spotted Tilly and Willy. Willy is almost as big as his mama now, and I couldn't help but smile.

"Storm, I want you to meet someone," I said, slowing. Storm stopped and looked at me, then at what I was looking at. His eyes grew big as the two massive whales swam toward us.

"This is Tilly, and she is sacred to us. She saved so many lives with your grandpa. That's why she has this scar." I pointed it out. He ran his hand down it, and we watched in amazement as it disappeared.

Holy shit.

"Healer," Titan whispered. I looked at him with curiosity. "Once every thousand years, a healer is born into the Mermaid race. The clan they are born into will be blessed for thousands of years."

"So a god, a healer, and a pure white cub. Damn," Takar said.

Damn is right.

"They age and mature quickly, so he will grow rapidly until the equivalent of twelve years old, then they slow until age eighteen when aging stops," Poseidon added. "I should add that once you mark her as a godly mate, she will also stop aging along with you."

"Well, no time to waste. We have a crowd that is ready to meet the prince."

We headed to the castle and swam to our thrones. Storm was now in my arms, feeling a bit tired from the swim.

"My beautiful Merfolk, as your god, I am pleased to announce the arrival of your MerPrince. Your prince is touched by the Pearl Goddess herself. His Highness is not only of godly descent but also a healer," Poseidon said.

Everyone spun with their excitement. Raf took Storm from my arms and held him just over his shoulders for everyone to see. Storm smiled as he seemed to take in the crowd. Gasps filled the waters as a white light spread out, surrounding everyone and circling a few specifically. Including Kai.

"He is healing the ill," Poseidon said in my mind.

Fascinating.

"Thank you all for coming, and thank you to the visiting council for joining us as well. We will travel to you soon and spread our good fortune."

Chapter Ninety-Three

TAKAR

Storm was full of so much energy, not to mention just how fast he was growing. He was born just a year ago, yet he was already a five-year-old in appearance but much older in ability. He took to his teachings and excelled at everything. I was having a hard time keeping up.

My parents visited often and even told us Rajiv had found his mate. I was so happy for him, and of course I would meet her when Aria and I finally got married tomorrow. We'd been so busy that planning our human wedding had fallen low on the priority list.I was staying at my old place while Aria was in a bridal suite at a beachside hotel.

She wanted the traditional "don't see each other," so I gave it to her.

Storm was staying with the nannies and his personal guard. This wedding was grand and not cheap by any means, but it was worth it.

Besides, business was booming.

I flopped down on my couch and sighed. This was the first time in a long time that I was spending the night alone. I missed her so much it hurt.

What the fuck is wrong with me?

"She is your other half. It's normal to feel attached," my dad said. "Hell, I was like this for a long time after I ran from your mom. I wouldn't say it went away. I just learned to manage it." He patted my shoulder. "You will see her tomorrow in whatever stunning dress she picked out."

"Yeah, I already know she will look absolutely stunning, but we haven't been apart since we mated. Slash is restless."

"Understandable, but it's one night. Plus, with your titles, it might not be the only night."

I let out a sigh. "Yeah, I know."

"Now let's go out and have some fun. I need to see this town you have spent years living in."

It didn't take us long to get to the club. Cora made sure we went to different ones so no one would see each other.

As mated shifters, we elected to avoid a strip club, and instead chose one with just loud music and dancing. I had frequented this club and regularly picked up women to take home before I met my mate.

Hopefully, I didn't run into any of my old flings. I did not need my dad knowing how much of a sleaze I had been.

We were led to the VIP area, and a "Groom" sash was placed on me. The server came over and gave us a bottle of champagne and a bottle of whiskey. Zaz wasted no time pouring the whiskey into the various glasses. Figures.

I downed mine, and it was immediately refilled.

"To my best friend and now, um, boss. Congrats," Zaz said. Everyone raised their glass and downed their shots.

"Isn't that the girl who got you off last time we were here?" Raf linked.

I looked over and grimaced. "Yeah."

"Well, she looks like she wants to talk."

Great, just what I need. "Not interested."

Before anyone could do anything, she was right up against the VIP ropes.

"Hey baby, remember me? How about we go for round two?" she said in what I assumed was her seductive voice. I looked at her like she had three heads.

"How about… no."

"Was my mouth not to your liking? I can rock your world with my bare pussy if you want."

I clenched my jaw, and that was the only cue my people needed.

"He said no, you need to leave," Zaz sneered.

"Oh please. You can't handle me." She let out a scoff. "You have to send your guard dogs. You can answer."

Excuse me, but I'm pretty sure I did.

"Last I checked, he said no. So back off," Zaz barked.

"Make me," she snarled.

With that, my dad stood and moved over to the girl.

"I would choose your next steps carefully. You have no idea who he is nor what he is capable of. So, I suggest you leave on your own. Since you are willfully unobservant and missed both his answer and the large sash across his chest, he is a groom, so taken. Your blowjob clearly wasn't that good if he didn't come back for more. You are nothing more than a harlot, a disgrace to the gods."

"Fuck you," she sneered.

"Nah, I don't do harlots, plus I'm taken as well by his mother and I am his father, so tread carefully," my dad threatened.

"What seems to be the issue here?" a bouncer asked.

"This person is not taking no as an answer, and I fear for my boss's safety outside of the VIP area with her around," Raf said.

Damn. And just like that, she was removed and trespassed from the club. I couldn't help but smirk. Even in the human world, my guard found ways to keep me safe but not reveal our secrets, even if they all wanted to take her head off.

I felt eyes on me and turned to see my father.

"How many?" was all he asked.

"Here, a lot, but not since Aria. And I don't think the rest will be an issue."

"Better not be."

Chapter Ninety-Four

ARIA

I was definitely restless being away from Takar and my baby, but I knew tomorrow would make everything worth it.

We were at a club that was unlike anything I had ever experienced before. The lights were bright, and the music was so loud I was vibrating.

I had never been to a club before, and I wasn't sure how I would like it. So far, the only thing I could think of was coming back here with Takar and having him take me on a vibrating speaker.

The VIP section was nice, and we immediately got champagne and wine.

"To the bride, my best friend. The bitch that changed my life forever, but of course for the better. We love you," Cora said.

We held up our glasses of red wine and took a sip.

"Looks like you have some admirers," Ursa said.

I saw two men staring our way. They weren't bad looking by any means, and before Takar I might have talked to them, but I was beyond happy and very much taken.

Once they noticed us looking, they walked toward us and stopped at the rope. "You ladies care for some company?" the tall one asked.

"No, thank you. It's my bachelorette party," I said politely.

"Well, you aren't married until tomorrow, so how about some fun?" the shorter one asked.

I just stared at him, flabbergasted. Ursa was in his face in the blink of an eye.

"If only you knew who you were talking to, who she was about to marry. Back the fuck off, or you will see just what I am capable of- and I am nothing compared to her groom," she threatened.

For a moment, I didn't think the message was received, but as security headed our way, they bolted.

"Now that the trash took itself out, let's enjoy the night," Cora said.

"Yes, let's." I turned back to enjoy the party.

Tomorrow couldn't come fast enough.

Chapter Ninety-Five

ARIA

Ursa and Cora fussed with my hair and makeup while I just sat there. Every time I moved, I was swatted and told to sit still. Then, of course, my mind would wander to my soon-to-be husband doing the same thing to me.

I let out a sigh and sank back deeper into the chair.

"Oh, stop your whining. We're almost done," Cora said. When they finally stepped back, I looked in the mirror.

I looked stunning. My hair was in a messy updo, and strands of hair framed my face. Shells lined the bun, making it look elegant.

Takar's mom walked in right on time with my dress.

When I went dress shopping, I hated all of them. I wanted a piece of me in my dress. When I found a seamstress willing to make a custom gown, I was so damn excited.

I stepped into the dress, and Cora and Ursa held it open for me. Cora walked me to the full-length mirror, and I gasped.

The iridescent ocean blue shimmered in the light. White lace that looked like waves made up the trim. The back dipped to the top of my butt while the front dipped to just above my belly button. A thin strap looped around my shoulder, then an off-the-shoulder sleeve completed the look.

"Beautiful," Takar's mom said.

I smiled and did a quick spin. My crown was placed on my head with my veil, and I was officially ready to go. As if right on cue, Titan walked in the door with a huge smile on his face.

"You look absolutely stunning," he said.

"Thanks," I replied.

"Shall we?" He held out his elbow.

With one last look in the mirror, I took his arm and headed out the door toward the garden where we were having our ceremony.

Once at the top of the spiral stairs, still hidden behind a curtain, I took a deep breath. The smell of the beach just beyond the garden combined with the scent of the flowers was a blend I never knew I needed.

My bridesmaids and Takar's groomsmen walked down the grand stairs, and now it was my turn.

Titan placed his hand on mine. "Destiny awaits."

The curtain drew back, and my eyes immediately zeroed in on Takar's. His gasp was audible. The hunger in his eyes sent a chill down my spine. Oh, I was in for it later.

He wore the tux well, and my mouth watered knowing what was hiding under all that material. As my eyes wandered, I noticed his bulge, and my breathing hitched. Was he so big now that it was that noticeable, or was he getting hard looking at me?

Fuck me.

Chapter Ninety-Six

TAKAR

I smirked when I saw her spot my bulge. It was very noticeable, and it didn't help that the stunning goddess in front of me turned me the fuck on. I was fighting to keep control of myself and not give her my godly mark right now in front of everyone.

Titan held out her hand and bowed his head as I took it. I wanted to pull her to me so badly, but it wasn't time.

Not yet.

But if she thought I wasn't going to kiss the breath out of her, she was mistaken.

"We are gathered here today to watch the union…"

I lost myself in her eyes, tuning out the words. Zaz elbowed me, and I blinked.

"Bro, say I do," he linked.

Oh shit

"I do," I said, and Aria smiled.

"I do," she said.

As the officiant started to say, "You may kiss the bride," I had

Aria pulled to my chest. I cupped her cheek and leaned down to take her lips with mine.

My tongue ran against her lips, begging for more access, and when she gave it, I dove right in. Fuck, she tasted so damn good. My hand gripped her hair in a fist, and I let out a moan.

The sound of Zaz clearing his throat and a slap on my shoulder from Raf made me release her lips. I turned and glared at him like I was going to kill him. He laughed and shook his head.

"Wait until later, dude," he linked.

I grumbled, and Aria let out a laugh.

"Hmm, seems that my King is a bit horny," she hummed in my mind, my cock leaking at the unspoken promises.

"Oh, after this reception, your body is mine all night long."

"Is that a threat, my King?"

"No, Maid, a promise."

Chapter Ninety-Seven

ARIA

After the ceremony, everyone headed to the reception while the photographer took some wedding photos. Storm was so damn handsome in his mini suit.

Takar held my hand as we headed to join our friends and family.

"Ah, look who it is," Takar said.

Raj approached with a stunning woman at his side, his mark visible on her shoulder.

"I see you found your mate," I said.

"Yes, my goddess. This is Jezebel. Jezebel this is Takar and Aria, the god and goddess I told you about," he said proudly.

"It is very nice to meet you. We hope you will make the journey to our lands soon," I said as I reached out my hand. She gave a quick bow, then shook my hand.

"Please, the pleasure is mine. And I look forward to it."

We continued to make our rounds, and I was getting tired, though there was no going to bed tonight.

Storm was with the guard and the nannies for the next few days, while Takar and I had a mini-honeymoon.

Ursa would use her powers to place us in the ocean just off the coast of Italy.

"Are you ready to go?" Takar asked.

"Yes, but I want to say goodbye to Storm first."

"I wouldn't have it any other way."

Once we found Storm, I gave him lots of hugs and kisses until he zapped me, telling me to go and he would be fine. His body was five, but his mind was older.

Cheers erupted as Takar and I headed to the beach, where Ursa was waiting. She took my dress, then handed me a more comfortable outfit before doing her thing.

When I blinked, I was a mermaid and in a new ocean.

Damn.

We made our way to a secluded spot on the shore and headed to our beach home. It was a gift from Poseidon. He said it was once his home, but he had no need for it now, so it was ours.

Gorgeous was not close to the right word for this place. It was so much more than that. It was a forest or rocks and trees. Sand as soft as satin and the air crisp. The house was made of stone that shimmered in the light. The castle-like corners made it seem more medieval but the arched windows made it modern.

Once inside, I turned to my husband and my body shuddered at the pure, unfiltered lust staring back.

I stumbled into the wall, and Takar was pinning me in a place in seconds.

"You are mine in every way except one. Tonight, you will become my fated goddess," he growled, just before slamming his lips to mine.

Oh, fuck me.

Chapter Ninety-Eight

TAKAR

The amount of control I had over my body was faltering. I needed to mark her the last way I could, and I needed to do it now.

My dad said my body would take over and do what I needed to, and I had a feeling this was part of that.

I picked her up and carried her up the stairs before gently tossing her onto the soft mattress. A deep growl escaped my lips, and my cock was as hard as I thought it could ever get.

In seconds, I had my clothes off as well as hers.

My cock leaked, the tip so purple I was getting concerned. I wanted to eat that sexy pussy, but right now, my cock needed its release. I needed to mark her, then I could take her any way I wanted all night long.

Without a word, I drove my length into her, making her arch her back and let out a sultry moan. A moan that almost had me cumming right then and there.

Not giving her time to adjust, I pulled out, then thrust back in.

"Oh fuck," she moaned.

My cock dove in and out of her like my life depended on it. Electricity seemed to flow between us, and I felt energized like never before. A tidal wave shot through me as my cock exploded in a whole new way. Cum slipped out, dripping down to her ass. I leaned down and kissed her just above her heart. When I lifted my head, a lion's head wrapped in an ocean wave was left behind.

My godly mark.

She kissed me in the same spot, making the mark appear just above my heart as well. My body jolted again, and I exploded deep inside her. I had no clue where all this cum was coming from, but fuck me.

Her body shook as she squirted, and I growled possessively before pulling out of her to get a taste. My eyes rolled back. It was sweet, spicy, mouthwatering, and made only for me.

Fucking heaven.

And once I had her clean, I was going to claim her over and over until our honeymoon was over.

We were not leaving this bed for anything, and I mean anything.

Slash came forward and roared, "Mine."

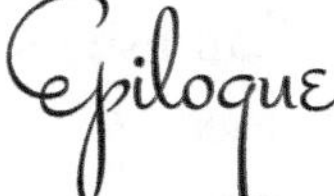

Epilogue

PEARL

I hated having to watch my daughter's wedding from a distance. Unfortunately, until she was marked fully, she was not permitted to see me.

Obviously, I let her have her honeymoon and stayed clear for that. No mother in her right mind wanted or needed to see that.

There was so much to tell her, to reveal to her. Mainly that my death was not in the plans, and technically neither was her father's, but despite everything, she still fulfilled her destiny and soon her son would too.

People thought my name, Pearl, came to be because my parents were pearl finders. Though that is partially true, it was told to them by me as I came to earth—well sea—through them.

I waited in the ocean as Takar, my son-in-law, and my daughter shifted and dove down.

As I tried to speak, the words fell short on my lips.

She was so damn beautiful.

Takar noticed me first and smiled.

"You look familiar somehow," he said.

I smiled. He had never met me, but he was mated to my daughter.

"No, you have not met me before, but you do know my daughter," I linked to him, and he gasped.

That got Aria's attention, and she looked in my direction.

"M-Mom," she said, stunned.

"Yes, my dear child, it is me."

"But you were, you're—"

"Dead. My human form is dead, but not my godly form."

"Godly?" Takar asked.

"I am the Pearl Goddess. The reason many in your clan received the pearl is because of me."

Aria was in my arms in seconds as she sobbed into my chest.

I didn't move. I didn't speak. I just held her there.

After a while, we caught up on everything. Now I had two things left.

"I came for a reason. One, your dad will visit soon. He was marked by me years ago, so he took his god form. He wanted to be here today, but he had duties that, unfortunately, could not wait. We will be around often."

She screamed out her delight and squeezed me into yet another hug.

"The last thing is a message I was sent to deliver."

"Okay," she whispered.

"Scales and Scars together make a Storm. A Storm of Healing and a Storm of Freedom. Fights with wolves and other enemies will come and could be Merkind's undoing, but the key to winning is the Storm within. Fear the unknown, but don't fear the unknown Storm as the key to triumph is deep within. The eye of the Storm is the most deadly."

I saw the confusion and I smiled.

"All will make sense when the time is right. Protect the Storm and all will thrive," I said as I disappeared from before them.

Bonus Chapter

DURING PARTS OF CHAPTERS 13-15

CORA

My mate held my hand. It didn't seem real, but here we were. Last night we talked a lot before we claimed each other.

For one, I had to tell him I wasn't human, that I was a mermaid. Then I had to tell him what a mate bond was and all that stuff. Once he had that knowledge, I let him pick what he wanted to do. And the rest is history.

Unfortunately, we couldn't just enjoy the bliss since he got a work call that couldn't wait. So now he was heading in, and I would hang with Aria until later.

One of the many things we talked about was what he did for work. He also told me everything he and Takar were doing to change things from the inside, which was all we could ever ask.

Aria might have some issues, but once it was all explained, she should be okay.

I hope.

We were walking up to the building when I saw Takar standing there alone, his facial expression making him look three times his age, his eyes haunted by something. I didn't see Aria anywhere.

The hell?

"Where is Aria?" I asked.

His eyes shifted to mine, then looked to Raf, his shoulders slumped like they were weighed down.

"I don't know," he whispered. I barely heard him, and his voice was so full of sadness and confusion it made my heart ache.

Crap

"Tell me everything."

"We… um… had fun all night and this morning. Then we came here. And out of nowhere, she just… took off."

As I looked around, I noticed the company sign, then it hit. This was *the* company.

Shit, this complicated matters.

Takar worked for the company responsible for her father's illness, her father's impending death, and so much devastation. That was different from working for the industry in general. This was going to take work to get through. I just hope the bond is strong enough. Though being unmarked can make it even harder.

Damn it.

I looked Takar in the eye. "Can you deal with whatever you need to do without Raf?"

He seemed to think for a minute before answering. "Yes."

"I *will* get her back. You just have to trust me."

His nod was slow, like his head was too heavy to move. I faced my mate. "I need you to explain what you said to me. This company poisoned and killed many of us. Including her father, who is fighting its effects and will soon pass. This is very raw for her."

Before he could answer, Takar spoke defensively. "I had nothing to do with that accident. I knew something was off about it but can't prove anything. Been fighting the system since."

I put my hands up in surrender.

"Easy there," I said, trying to calm him. "You know Aria and I are mermaids, right?"

When he nodded, I continued. "We have a counterpart called sirens. They are the devil's version of us. Sirens use spelled music to lure ships to their death, which is what happened with your company. Our MerSoldiers tried to stop it, her father leading the interception. But they were too late. We lost so many men, and the ones who lived are slowly dying. One being her father, who is an important man to our kind. Losing him will be devastating if Aria isn't mated. I know you didn't work there at the time, but you are associated with them now. "

As I spoke, his shoulders seemed to get heavier, his eyes filled with tears, and his lips fell into a deep frown. I could see the utter devastation all over his body. I placed my hand on his arm, making him look up at me. "I've got this."

Once Takar nodded, I grabbed Raf's hand and led him to a secluded spot on the beach. When we got there, I pulled him to me and brushed my lips over his. "I know this isn't how we planned this. Hell, I wanted your first shift to be romantic and show you the beautiful ocean. But Aria needs us, and in order for you to help, you have to shift now. I promise I will give you the experience I wanted you to have, but it will have to wait."

He cupped my cheek in his palm and smiled. "She is my best friend's mate and my mate's best friend. I will do anything to help."

I let out a relieved sigh. "Okay. I need you to close your eyes and walk with me to the ocean." I guided him to the water until we were waist-deep. "Now picture yourself with a tail and command your body to shift. Remember, this will hurt, but only the first time."

He did as I instructed. Soon his body was twisting and shifting, making him groan in pain. As soon as I knew he was okay, I shifted and told him to open his eyes.

Once we were fully underwater, I had to hold back a laugh when I noticed Raf holding his breath. "Raf, sweetheart, you can breathe underwater."

He looked at me skeptically, but let out his breath and smiled once he realized I was right. "This is amazing."

"I know, but we don't have time for you to enjoy your new form. Right now, we have a job to do."

"Of course."

I took a few minutes to help him figure out how his tail worked. Thankfully, it didn't take much since he had been a swimmer in high school. He followed me as I swam toward the city. First place I looked for her was her house. Nothing said she was there or had even been there recently.

Next, the hospital where her father was. I went up to the front desk and checked in with the clerk. "She was here, but left a little while ago."

"Thank you," I said, then went to one last place. The place she and I used to hang out as kids when we needed to get away and just be. Raf didn't say much, just squeezed my hand every chance he could. Our bond allowed me to feel how worried he was.

As we went into the clearing, my eyes roamed the vast reef in search of my friend. It was eerily quiet, and my guess was the fish knew something was up. Despite what humans may think, fish are quite intelligent.

Seaweed flowed as the water swirled, and I finally saw her sitting on some coral near the reef's edge. I let out a relieved breath, then turned to Raf. "Wait here. Let me talk to her first, then I will motion for you to come over when we are ready."

"Okay," he whispered, then gave me a quick kiss.

I swam over and sat next to her. She looked at me and let out a sigh.

"Talk to me, A."

"There isn't much to say, C. He works for the people responsible for my father and so many others."

Her tone was one of devastation. I had no clue if I could fix this, but I was going to at least try. "What if I told you he wasn't the bad guy? Yes, he works for the bad guy, but he is doing good."

She raised an eyebrow. I pointed to Raf, and she looked over in his direction, then back at me.

"Last night when we were getting to know each other, he told me how he worked for an oil company, though not by name, or I would have warned you. He told me how they worked together and were making changes for the good. When we got to the beach this morning, Takar was shattered and confused," I said as I watched her body language.

It was clear she was listening, so I took the opportunity to wave Raf over. He explained every little thing they were doing and had done, and she continued to listen.

"I just…I don't know. I mean, obviously we are mates, and despite not being marked, it is strong. Staying mad at him is not an option. But right now, I just need space. I need time to process all of this in my own way."

"Understandable. Go be with your dad. We will see you soon," I said before grabbing Raf's hand and heading back to shore.

Once we got to shore, we shifted. His shift back was smooth and practically painless. Not to mention hot as hell. I pulled him into me.

"I'm sorry this wasn't the magical experience I hoped it would be," I whispered into his chest.

"Don't be. You know Takar is like a brother to me. I will do anything for him, and if that means not getting to enjoy my first shift, then that is a sacrifice I am willing to make."

I opened my mouth to reply when his phone rang.

"Hello," he said into the speakerphone.

"Takar…okay…I'm…safe…away…soon," a broken male voice said before the line went dead.

What the hell?

No, wait, who the hell?

I looked at Raf like he had three legs.

"We need to find Takar, now," he said in a voice of urgency.

"I'm guessing the office since you guys got called in," I replied. He grabbed my hand and started walking toward the office. "Baby, what's going on?"

"That was our friend, our brother-in-arms. He has been MIA, but I guess not anymore," he said, as his joy and relief radiated from his eyes as they landed on my own. "Knowing his relationship with Takar, he might be able to help with this mess."

Fuck, I hope so.

When we arrived at the office, Takar looked up with hope in his eyes, only to slump into the chair as he realized we did not have his mate with us.

"Takar, you still have to trust me. She knows the truth, but needs some time to process it all. I know she will be back," I said softly. He nodded, but I could tell he was still struggling with all of this.

"Hey man. I can't imagine your feelings right now, but I have good news," Raf said. Takar glanced up with questions all over his features. "Did you turn off your phone?"

"Yeah, I needed quiet."

"Well, when he couldn't reach you, he called me."

"Who?"

"Zaz."

"Zaz," he exclaimed. "He's…"

"Alive, yes. And he will be home soon from what I could catch. His reception was terrible."

Takar's face was a blend of happy and broken. Torn between his brother and his mate.

This shit sucked.

There wasn't anything else we could do, so we left to give him space. Once outside, I walked into Raf's chest.

"I'm going to go talk to Aria. I will see you tonight."

Raf brushed my hair behind my ear and pulled me in for a sweet kiss. "Go help your friend. I'm not going anywhere."

With one last kiss, I headed back to Aria.

Acknowledgments

To Good Girl Author Services: Thank you so much for all you have done for me. I can't thank you enough. Even after every set back I have had with this book, you always come through for me.

To Emily Michel: Thank you for being this book's saving grace. Your TikTok video saved me from panic after losing my previous editor. I can't thank you enough.

To K.B. Barrett Designs: I am so glad I found you through **Jade Dollston.** Thank you for getting me on your busy schedule and making my cover come to life.

To everyone else who's helped: There are many others I have met on BookTok and Facebook who have been amazing and helped with small little things along the way. There are so many I can't possibly list them all. Just know you are appreciated.

About the Author

Between her part-time job in the security industry, her full-time job in healthcare admin, and being a mom of three boys, Cierra finds the time to write all things smut. At any given time, she can have multiple books in progress and the list of future books could be its own novella. She's loved writing from a young age, and with her mom being a reporter, you could argue it's in her blood. While sitting in the hospital with one of her boys after his brain surgery, she wrote her first book. Next thing she knew, she was five books deep and editing her debut from those five. She dabbles in shifters, vampires, humans, fairies, witches, first responders, and so much more. Pay careful attention while reading—she leaves Easter eggs for future books.